Cortijo, Luis
'44'

CHINA SKY

CHINA SKY

by Pearl S. Buck

TRIANGLE BOOKS

New York

TRIANGLE BOOKS EDITION PUBLISHED NOVEMBER, 1942

By arrangement with THE JOHN DAY COMPANY, INC.

REPRINTED NOVEMBER 1942
REPRINTED JANUARY 1943
REPRINTED APRIL 1943
REPRINTED JUNE 1943
REPRINTED AUGUST 1943
REPRINTED DECEMBER 1943

Because of the acute shortage of regular book cloth under
war-time rationing, this book is bound in "leatherette," a
sturdy paper fabric especially designed for this purpose.

TRIANGLE BOOKS, 14 West Forty-ninth Street
New York, N. Y.

PRINTED IN THE UNITED STATES OF AMERICA
AMERICAN BOOK—STRATFORD PRESS, INC., NEW YORK

CHINA SKY

THE LONG WAIL of the first air-raid warning of the night shrieked through the unlighted Chinese city and rebounded from the darkening hills outside its walls.

"Thank you," Sara said to the blue-coated coolie from the cable office. She had been in the women's ward to see a patient upon whom she had operated that day when she had heard her name called from the door, and there was this cable. She thrust it into the pocket of her white surgical coat. There was no time to read even a cable—no time, either, to go to the hospital office and open the cash box and get a tip for the coolie.

"You had better go into our shelter until this is over," she said. "The Japanese come quickly these days." The length of the long city lay between the hospital and the cable office on the river.

The man hesitated and then shook his head. "I have a new American bicycle. It will be too quick for those Japs. As for what you are thinking of, do not remember it. Take it for my thanks to you that you do not leave us as many white women do."

He darted off, and Sara hurried to the top floor, smiling. She must remember to give him something all the same. . . . Babies were on the top floor, and the new mothers. They were always first.

"Everybody to his place," she said quietly as she went, speaking to one after another of the Chinese orderlies and nurses who, as they had been taught, appeared along the corridors. At the sound of her voice they disappeared. Within five minutes all the hospital seemed to be moving down the ramps out into the soft autumn night. Everything was dark except for the enormous hanging moon, "a beacon to the Japanese," Sara thought bitterly, upstairs in the baby room. By the light of a broad moonbeam falling through an open window she lifted one tiny form after another from its cradle and tucked it into a long wagonlike carriage she had designed especially for this purpose. The Japanese had been bombing Chen-li so long that she had had time to invent every means of this sort. Only the sure-to-dies were left behind in an air raid now—those who, if they were moved at all, would die the sooner.

The second warning sounded. She glanced out of the window. Across the dark and rocky hills a long thin line of flickering lights was moving, lights as small as fireflies. But they were not fireflies. They were flashlights held by thousands of people from the city who were going to the caves in the cliffs. She had seen them hundreds of times by daylight, mothers with their babies on their backs, and in their hands baskets of food and little three-legged stools. The floors of the caves were wet from the dripping roofs. But the rock was seventy feet thick over their heads.

"Off with you," Sara said in English to the tiny Chinese babies. Two blue clad Chinese nurses wheeled them quickly away. But she always packed the babies herself, ever since that awful night, now nearly a year ago, when one of them had been smothered. She and Gray had worked hours over that small motionless mite while bombs crashed around them. It was certain even then that the Japanese wanted to hit the hospital. It had been hit again and again. But they always patched it up. Ah, but she was tired! Five months she had been here alone while Gray was in America getting money to go on patching up the hospital. After the war he was going to tear down the whole patched-up pile, he said, and build an up-to-date modern American hospital and let Chen-li see what a hospital really was.

If the war ever ended!

"Mothers all out?" Sara asked of a young Chinese woman who was waiting.

"Everybody is out except the eight sure-to-dies you said were not to be moved—and you," the young woman replied.

She stood immobile in her white intern's uniform.

3

Sara laughed. "Now, Siu-mei, you need not look at me like that, for it is you who go and I who stay. Hurry and catch up with the babies. You must be with them in the shelter."

"No, Elder Sister!" Siu-mei cried out. "If I die, there are others like me, but who will take your place? Thomison doctor is far away in America. We have only you."

"Nobody can kill me," Sara said gaily. The third siren sounded, and immediately heavy planes drummed across the sky. "Quick—quick!" she screamed soundlessly. But the Chinese girl did not move. She took Siu-mei by the shoulders and pushed her toward the door. It was no use. The girl was strong and stubborn, and she turned and clutched Sara.

"Here—in the door!" she shrieked. They stood, their heads bent, their mouths open to relieve the tension of the fearful roar around them. The planes dived downward until it seemed from the noise that they would crash through the roof. Automatically the two women crouched and hung their heads between their knees and pressed their fingers in their ears.

The bomb fell. There was an explosion that shattered the air and dried it up so that they could scarcely breathe. Then there was the crash of falling walls. Sara lifted her head.

"That's the wing of the men's ward," she said, but

4

her voice was still soundless. Siu-mei pushed down her head.

"It is not over!" she shrieked.

They crouched, waiting. Three times more the planes dived; three times the air seemed dried up around them. Sara put her hands upon her breast to ease it so that she could draw the breath that was sucked out of her lungs. Then she remembered the cable. There it was, still in her pocket where she had thrust it. No time yet for anything except this life-and-death business! But what if it were from Gray? Only why should Gray cable her when he had written his plans out so carefully in his cool, businesslike letters? And everything, he said, was going according to plan. There was no urgency in Gray to communicate with her.

The planes receded somewhat. She leaped to her feet.

"I must see to the sure-to-dies," she told Siu-mei. "Now go, you, and see what is happening in the shelter."

She hurried ahead without waiting for answer, her small pencil flashlight guiding her feet. Into the men's ward first—that young Chinese doctor fresh from American medical school was taking Gray's place there, but she could not be sure of him. He was never quite to be found either in his place or exactly out of it. "I don't trust Dr. Chung," she had written Gray recklessly in one of the letters that she tried to make nothing but reports, "and I can't say why."

"Don't go feminine on me," he had written back

sternly. "Chung came with a brilliant record and recommendations beyond anything *I* ever had."

But tonight Dr. Chung was in his place in the men's ward. A pencil of light crossed hers, and his face came into her sight as hers came to his.

"What was hit?" she asked.

"The west corner, doctor," he said calmly. "Too bad, when we've just finished repairing it."

"That makes you short of beds, doesn't it?" She held his smooth oval face in the light. His black eyes looked flat and opaque.

"Eight men with no beds to come back to, doctor."

"Pallets in the dining hall."

"Yes, doctor."

She wished he would not "doctor" her so much. He was still displeased that Gray had put her in charge of the hospital when he went to America. Gray had been so angry that he had told her what Chung had said.

"A woman!"

"No, my colleague, Dr. Sara Durand," Gray had replied haughtily.

"A woman," the Chinese had insisted sullenly.

"I wanted to hit the fellow," Gray had told her. "But I didn't dare—not when I've got to leave. Better watch your step, Sara!"

She had watched her every step, ignoring Chung's sullenness and the edges of rudeness in his manner. It was difficult to tell what was rudeness in these modern young Chinese, who purposely put aside the traditions of Chinese courtesy as old-fashioned and yet did not know what Western courtesy was.

"Is there anything else?" she asked.

"I can manage, thank you, doctor." Again the flicker of insolence in the smooth bland voice and in the long handsome black eyes.

"Very well—good night, Dr. Chung."

"Good night, Dr. Durand."

She let his face go and turned and was aware of fear. As surely as she could see it she felt the needlepoint of his light upon her back. He was watching her. Instantly she turned and flung her light at him. He had not moved.

"What is it?" she demanded.

His narrow eyes widened. "I was merely casting my light on your path," he said gently.

She was ashamed of herself as she shut the door between them.

"I'm overwrought," she thought. "I'm beginning to imagine things. It is time Gray came back."

She put her hand to her pocket and felt the crackle of paper. When she had one moment—but she had not, yet! Five of the sure-to-dies were in the women's ward, and she must get around before the patients came back from the shelter. There would be plenty to do then— people exhausted and needing stimulants and children needing food.

7

She hurried into the ward where two women lay motionless, a few empty beds between. Were they—? No, they were alive. Two heads turned weakly, and one of the women put out a hand.

"I knew you would come, foreigner. They don't hit foreigners, do they?"

"Everybody is safe," Sara said quietly, putting thermometers into mouths. Even as she spoke the siren sounded again for safety. It was over again for the night—for a few hours—perhaps even for a day, until tomorrow night. She glanced out of the window toward the hills. Out of the caverns the tiny firefly lights were beginning to waver down the slopes. People were going back to their beds. Her eyelids suddenly burned with tears. They were so brave, these Chinese people, so uncomplaining, so unyielding. Day in, day out, night after night, they endured this horrible life, shifting their hours of work patiently to meet necessity, nobody grumbling, not a word of yielding to the enemy.

"A people worth giving my life to," she thought, with that mingling of tenderness and determination which was most herself. "I'm lucky," she thought. "So many have to work for bread alone—my bread is incidental."

She and Gray had talked about that.

"We're lucky," Gray had said. "Every moment here is worth living, and if you die, death's worth it, too."

She took out the thermometers. One was dangerously

8

subnormal, and she whipped out a hypodermic full of stimulant from the small emergency bag she carried. Otherwise these two were no worse.

"Rice gruel will come in a few minutes," she said. "Drink it and sleep in peace."

"Peace!" one of the women sighed.

"Buddha send us peace!" the other whispered.

"Peace will come," Sara promised. Somehow, sometime! What would it be like to live and work in peace again? Gray must tell her how it was at home, in America.

She visited two private rooms. In one a young woman was already healthily asleep. It was the woman she had operated on this afternoon. She took her temperature without waking her—it was near enough to the margin of safety.

It was only when she went into the last room that she found the woman on the high hospital bed was dead. She was a very old lady who had been brought in a week before, dying then.

"Let me die," she had said whenever Sara came in. "Why do you make me live?"

"I never let anybody die," Sara had answered, smiling into the small knot of an old face.

"It is time for me to die," the old woman always said.

Perhaps it was, Sara thought. She put down now the shriveled claw of a hand that she had taken up. This sort of death was not horrible—only peaceful. Peace!

Perhaps this was it. She felt suddenly very tired, and she sat down on the bench by the bed. In the bright light the little dead woman looked exactly as she had alive, except for the peace upon her face.

The hospital was now full of soft slurring noises. The patients were being brought back. She must move on since there was no more to be done here—move on to the living. But Siu-mei would be there looking after them all. She had a moment in which to rest.

And then she knew that all along she had been watching and waiting for the moment she had been too conscientious to take. She wanted it, not for rest, but to open the envelope in her pocket. But first, let her think, if it were not from Gray, then no disappointment! Gray had written her faithfully and regularly. There was no reason why a cable should come from him—unless he were postponing his return? If it were that—she was simply too tired.

"Oh, you big fool!" she cried to herself. "Go on, open it! Besides, you're never too tired to do your work. It is what you live for."

She tore the envelope open with fingers used to the resolution of the knife and read in the scrawling ill-formed letters of the Chinese clerk at the cable office these words from Gray:

Bringing my wife with me. Will you fix up south bungalow for us? Sorry to give short notice but things were sudden. Louise and I send thanks and best wishes. Gray.

Louise and I—Gray— Louise and I—Gray— Her eyes picked out the four incredible words, and she tortured herself with them. Louise and I—Gray— She tore the envelope into little bits and put them into the wastebasket by the bed. Who was Louise? She had been given no warning of her. But it was perfectly natural that Gray should marry.

"I must get to work," she thought quietly. She smoothed the covers over the little dead woman. "There's a lot for me to do," she thought.

She bit her lips and squared the corners of the bed. They were not disturbed. The old lady must have died quietly without moving. Perhaps the concussion had strangled her. Louise and I—Gray— But she and Gray were nothing but American colleagues in a Chinese hospital; never had been anything but that—never, never had Gray thought of loving her, he the most honorable of men, careful of her reputation, observing the minutest detail of behavior between a man and a woman in China so that no one could talk.

"We can't have our work cluttered up with gossip," he had said—Chinese always thought that men and women had to—she had been proud that she and Gray could show them that a man and woman could work side by side and remain friends and colleagues.

She fell suddenly to her knees and laid her head against the bed. They were right, these Chinese! They were always right, these people ages old—a man and woman couldn't—not a man like Gray and a woman like her.

"I love him," she thought, and took agony into her soul. "There is no use in pretending, no use in arguing."

She strained her body upward, not to pray, because no prayer was in her, only agony. But at that moment the door opened. Siu-mei put in her head.

"Elder Sister— Why, what is wrong? Are you praying?"

Sara rose to her feet. "This old one is dead," she said.

Siu-mei came into the room, surprise upon her pretty face. "It is a pity," she said, wondering, "but she was very old. And we are all waiting for you."

"I am ready," Sara said. "I was just coming."

. . . She went to her patients thinking rebelliously, "Has Gray forgotten what these days and nights are, that he asks me to arrange a house? When is there time for a house and ordinary living in it?"

One by one she tended sick women and talked to their frightened relatives, come to see if any were dead in the hospital. She saw that each little newborn child was tucked back into its cubicle of a bed and sent Lao Wang, the old hospital gardener, to call the family of the dead woman. Then she went back to her office to wait for their coming. Siu-mei was there ahead of her.

"Go to bed, Elder Sister," she said. "I will attend to the family. You are ill yourself."

"No, not ill," Sara replied. "Only tired—and who is not tired these days? You go, child. You do too much for me as it is."

"I will not," Siu-mei replied. Her face grew stubborn. "Such a pretty face," Sara thought in the passing instant. Siu-mei's prettiness was incongruous in these grim times. Besides, what was the use of a woman's being pretty? She herself—but it had been weeks since she had looked at her own face in a mirror to see it. Now it would never matter to her again how she looked.

"If they want someone other than you," she said yielding, "will you call me?"

Siu-mei shook her smooth black head. "I will not disturb you. I will call Dr. Chung."

She blushed faintly, and Sara saw it. It was impossible not to see it in the glare of the hard overhead light falling full upon the girl's pale clear skin. She was suddenly acutely sensitive with fatigue and sorrow, and at once aware of what was behind Siu-mei's blush. Words burned upon her tongue. "Ah, don't love anybody, Siu-mei!" But she did not speak them. She bowed her head.

"Very well, Siu-mei, thank you," she said.

. . . In her own rooms in the east wing of the hospital she did not turn on the lights. There was no need. The brilliant moon filled them with a soft amber glow, the Chinese moonlight of a September night, at once softer and brighter than any moonlight in the world. By its

13

light a ship was plowing its steady way across the sea, bringing Gray and his wife. She could see the little bungalow in the south corner of the compound from her window. After they came, after its windows were alight and its doors open, could she go on living here alone, looking down upon that life in which she had no part? The house had been built for the resident doctor—it was Gray's house. But he had wanted to live in the men's hospital, near his work. The very first day she had come, now nearly two years ago, he had pointed out the bungalow to her—a low, gray brick square, its roof tiled with black Chinese tiles.

"That's supposed to be my house, but I don't want it. I've got to be near my work," he had said.

She had thought it fine in him to want to be near his patients night and day, and cheerfully she had made her own three rooms a home for herself. But he had never been in them. Chinese custom forbade it, and he was rigorous in obeying that custom, even while he joked about it.

"It's a responsibility having my colleague a young and beautiful woman," he had said one day, smiling at her. "I never thought of such a thing. When I first saw you I was all upset."

"Was that why you looked at me so queerly when you met me?" she cried. "I thought you didn't like me."

"I was stunned! I hadn't thought of specifying middle-aged and plain when I asked for a woman doctor. It didn't occur to me that anything else could be found to come to a hospital fifteen hundred miles into the middle of China."

But she had leaped at the chance, even though Gray's letter had said: "Send me someone who can operate with anything, anywhere." She had just finished her internship at a Kansas City hospital, and she knew about China because there had been a lonely Chinese in her class and she had been sorry for him, and had gone with him sometimes to dine in a Chinese restaurant or to wander through the new Chinese art museum. There was something about the museum that drew her back to it again and again alone to look at the paintings of strange mountains and cliffs and waterfalls. She used to think, "There are no mountains like these." Yet there they were, outside of her windows now. But the old painters had never dreamed of painting across them that flickering line of firefly lights of the thousands of people going to shelter from the bombs of enemies.

So when the head doctor told them of the positions open, there was this one and she spoke up at once. "I'd like to go to China." No one else wanted it, and so it was easy enough. That is, until she went back to her home on a farm and to her family, to whom the very name of China was as far away as the stars.

"What on earth put that in your head?" her father demanded.

"I just want to go," she said.

15

They let her go, doubtfully because she was young and a woman, a little less doubtfully because they hadn't wanted her to be a doctor anyway—women doctors had a hard time getting started anywhere, and maybe China would be a good thing. So she had come, twenty-six, strong, eager, gay, ready for anything. Was she beautiful? Gray had said "young and beautiful." Anyway, she had dark hair and blue eyes and good skin. She was too tall, but not as tall as Gray. And what was this Louise, and how did she look, and how could Gray have written her nothing if he was falling in love and then sent only this cable, to prepare his home for him and his wife?

She sank upon the floor and put her arms upon the window sill and wept, and the full Chinese moon shone down upon her with a brightness that was so strong she felt it warm upon her flesh.

Then there came upon her at that moment a strange pressing sense of something inexorable rushing toward her, a ship moving swiftly across the sea toward her, the hour inevitably to come upon her, the life she must go on with. She rose to meet them all. She bathed and put on cool Chinese silk pajamas and brushed her long straight dark hair and braided it down her back. She lay upon her bed upon the fine woven mat placed for coolness over the sheet.

"I can do what must be done," she told herself. "When I love Gray so much, can I not do for him what he wants?"

But there was no use in pretending that sleep was possible to her rigid, tense body, and she lay waiting for the dawn.

. . . Four days later she gazed at the droning Japanese planes over the hospital again. There had been raids every day, every night. The hospital was full. Twenty-two sure-to-dies today, and she had pushed Siu-mei firmly down the ramp with the last of the ones who might live. Then she ran through the corridor into the men's hospital to find Dr. Chung. She would tell him to go to the shelter too. If Siu-mei were in love with him, it was important that he live. It was important that all love be kept alive. But he was not there. An old orderly in a faded blue uniform sat in the hall.

"Where's Chung doctor?" she cried.

"He is gone to the shelter with a rich patient," the old man said cheerfully. "He bade me stay behind in his place."

"Ah," Sara said. She went back displeased. A doctor had no right—then she checked herself. Even doctors were human. Siu-mei had gone willingly today, and could she blame these two for wanting to be safe? She stood under the arch of a door, waiting, and gazing out of the window opposite. Beside her was her emergency bag, ready with everything. Let them come!

"But they won't hit me," she thought desperately. "They'll hit Gray's house, sure. I wonder if the workmen are all out?" And Siao Fah—"Gray would never forgive me if anything happened to him," she thought. Siao Fah was Gray's cook-boy, a squat, pock-marked fellow from a near-by village. As soon as he had heard Gray was coming back, he had moved into the servants' quarters behind the bungalow and begun to clean his kitchen.

But it was too late to see to anything. The drone of the heavy enemy planes dived near to the earth, and she crouched and hung her head. There was the high scream of the lighter Chinese planes soaring and then plunging upon the enemy from above. She lifted her head—had to lift it to see this.

"Brave—brave!" she cried aloud. Two Chinese planes against twenty! The Chinese had so few planes that they sent up one—two—against the vicious flock beneath them. But the Chinese pilots were nimble and quick. Their small planes buzzed and darted and whirled, firing, evading, firing again. She ran to the window and shouted at them.

"Oh, brave—brave—brave!" she shouted. The enemy formation was breaking up, and whenever that happened the Japanese airmen became confused, and soon they would withdraw. But before that came about she saw a bomb drift down, veering a little in the wind. It was headed straight for Gray's house. She watched it, her hand to her mouth. Would the wind be strong enough to push it beyond the compound wall? It came down, a long silver slant, pointing a little to the south, a little more, enough. She put her hands to her ears and opened her mouth and felt the explosion all through her body. A great spray of earth and bricks flew up. But Gray's house was still safe. She saw it still whole, debris piled against it.

She went out after it was all over and the hospital ordered again and stepped into the house. The men were already back, plastering the walls, nailing down new boards where white ants had eaten away the floor, putting in new screens at the windows. Siao Fah was there to hasten them.

"You are all safe?" she inquired.

They laughed back at her for answer, and one of them spat on the board he was nailing down, and then, remembering that the floor was for a foreigner, wiped it off with the sole of his shoe.

"Thomison doctor's house will be ready, lady doctor," Siao Fah said. "Don't fret, don't excite yourself. You have said he comes in seven more days, and in seven more days all will be finished."

"Don't forget I must have furniture in and curtains up," she said. "Two days for that, if the Japanese allow it."

"The gods decide, not they," Siao Fah said calmly.

"I'm not so sure," she said.

"Ah, but we are," he replied.

She went away, full of that deep aching pain that was

19

with her now night and day. "I must get used to it," she thought. "I must just get used to it."

So she went out one rainy day between operations, a day when the good gray clouds protected the city, and bought for the price of American cheesecloth Chinese figured silk to make curtains for Gray's house and clean straw-colored matting for the floors and plain heavy Chinese furniture. She piled everything on rikshas and took one herself and followed her caravan back to the hospital. And that evening she measured and cut, and the hospital sewing women came and helped her and Siao Fah sweated and pushed the furniture into place. And so the house grew under her hands into Gray's home. And the next day, before the air-raid hour, she went with two hospital coolies and Siao Fah into Gray's rooms and watched them take Gray's things out of this place where he had lived alone into the house where he would live with Louise. It was the first time she had ever been in his rooms. She stood there looking at his belongings, which she had never seen, his books, his few pictures. The two of his parents she had seen. He had brought them to her one day.

"These have just come," he told her. "They are my mother and father."

She had studied the handsome old faces, very gentle faces, his mother's delicate and too sensitive. "They were wonderful when I told them I was coming to China," he said tenderly. "I might as well have said I was going to die. I'm their only one, you know. But they told me to go ahead."

She had grown up in a brimming houseful of children, a bustling farmer her father. "Don't see why Kansas isn't good enough for any child of mine," he had grumbled, and grumbled in every letter to this day.

And Louise—would she be like Gray, the child of plenty and peace? Gray's rooms were simple and plain, but everywhere there were the signs of his parents' plenty —the sheets on his shelves were linen, and she had never slept between linen sheets in her life. In his closet a blue dressing gown had been forgotten, a heavy American silk with his initials monogrammed on the pocket. A folded silk handkerchief was in the pocket. She pulled it out and laid her cheek upon it. Gray's smell, clean and fragrant of piney soap, was in it still. "I'll keep it," she thought. Why not? He would not miss it—

Into the house went his things, his easy chair, his heavy Chinese table, his books. She was glad she had told the carpenter to build the bookcases. She opened the books, one after the other. Marco Polo, crisscrossed with his notes and queries; a Chinese *materia medica*, written by a missionary doctor; poetry and poetry again. She had no right—no, she would have no right when Louise came, but now Gray had asked her.

She came back the next night after the hospital was quiet and the rain still falling, a curtain of safety all day, and sat down in Gray's chair, and opened a book.

Everything was ready. If the house were not bombed in the next day or two days, or at utmost three days, he would come into it, into the home she had made for him. She had made it for him, for him alone, not for Louise. Oh, into the bedroom she had put another bed like his, and from an old furniture shop she had bought a small bride's table of blackwood and a carved stool. But everything else was for him.

But when he came in, she must go out. She had in these few days come to love running in and out of this house. It was sweet to open the door freely, to come in, to move a chair, a table, to examine the way a picture hung, to arrange a cushion, to imagine how it would look to Gray when he first saw it, to imagine—to imagine it was for Gray and for herself. She leaned back in Gray's chair and let herself imagine, his copy of Shelley open upon her knees. She could not read it, after all. She was too full of her own longings to read another's.

"I almost wish," she thought, "I do wish it—that a bomb would fall here and now—upon me, in this house."

. . . There was a loud crack of noise. She leaped, and the book fell from her knees with a crash. What was that? Not a bomb, of course—only a door, slammed shut. She heard a heavy step, and before she could rise a man stood in the doorway, a tall young Chinese in a torn blue uniform. The light of the shaded lamp fell upon his face and shadowed it, an angular, harsh, resolute face, youthful and strong.

"Who are you?" she asked.

"Are you the American woman doctor?" he demanded. She could see he was a man of authority.

"I am."

"Then come to the hospital. I have one there who must not die."

"If it is a man, the Chinese Chung doctor will take care of him. I care for the women."

"A Chinese cannot take care of this man," he said. "He is a Japanese."

"A Japanese!" she repeated. "But how—why do you, a Chinese, say a Japanese must not die?"

"I have my reasons," the young man said brusquely. "Come, woman doctor. There is no time to talk. He is bleeding."

She rose. "Nevertheless, he must go in the men's hospital," she said firmly.

"I care nothing of where he goes," the man said. "But you must be responsible for him."

He kept at her side as she walked through the dark rain. He had the small flashlight that every Chinese had these days and poured a moving pool of light upon their path.

"I cannot be responsible if the Japanese bomb the hospital, as they have many times, and he is killed among others," she said.

He agreed to that unwillingly. "No, for that alone I will not blame you. But if he dies in another way—if he is poisoned or made away with or if he bleeds to death or if—"

"He will not be murdered in my hospital, I can promise you," she said haughtily.

"Then you must make yourself responsible," he said sternly.

"Who are you?" she retorted. "How dare you come upon me in the middle of the night and command me as though I were your servant."

"I am Chen-ta, called the Eagle, and I am chief of the Tong Mountain guerrillas," he said.

Sara looked at the man again. So this was the Eagle! Who did not know him!

He went on, "This Japanese is my captive. We engaged the enemy four days ago in the northern part of the province, and him I took with my own hands, after I had wounded him. He is my prisoner."

"And you want me to cure him so that you may kill him more fully?" They were in the hospital now, and now in her office. She put on her surgical coat and began to scrub her hands.

"Do not waste time washing," he said impatiently.

"It is not waste," she said. "You do not understand these things."

But she made haste, for at that moment Siu-mei came into the room.

"Chung doctor has examined the Japanese and says he will operate, Elder Sister."

"That he will not!" the young man shouted. He put his hand on the knife of untempered iron at his girdle. "No one but this American woman shall touch him. He is mine, and I say this for a command."

"I will operate," Sara said evenly. "Do not excite yourself. Siu-mei, let the man be taken into my own operating room. Make him ready yourself. Ask Chung doctor to be ready to assist, but only if necessary." She turned to the young man. "Tell me quickly what is wrong."

"He is wounded in the belly," the chieftain said.

"With what?"

"With this." He pulled the thick-bladed knife out of his girdle.

"Did you stab him?"

"How else would he be mine? He was escaping, the fleetest foot I ever saw. I rushed at him sidewise. He tripped me and I fell, but I thrust him while I did it and ripped the side of his belly. Even so he was trying to escape, holding his belly together in his hands."

"A brave man, and therefore strong to survive," she said.

"He is no common man," the chieftain agreed.

She hurried into the hall, and he was close behind her.

"You cannot come into the room while I operate," she flung over her shoulder.

25

"I will come in," he declared. "It is my right to see that the man lives."

"I will not allow you in," she called back.

"Nevertheless, I will come," he maintained.

She let him come and let him stay when she saw the Japanese. There was no time to waste in argument. The man's life was flowing away in minutes and seconds with the blood that flowed from his side. She plunged her hands into disinfectant and drew on her rubber gloves and her mask. Around the table Siu-mei and Dr. Chung were ready, and two Chinese girl nurses held the instruments. She wavered for one instant about the anesthetic.

"Siu-mei, you," she said. Why did she not quite trust Chung? The chieftain, perhaps—he was standing there glowering at them from the corner. She wondered for an instant, waiting for the anesthetic, what he was thinking, used to death and violence. The mercy a knife could be was new. She took one quick look at him. His eyes were upon Siu-mei's face, absorbed in her task. He was staring at her, his black eyes unblinking.

"Ready," Siu-mei said clearly.

She picked up the shining scalpel and forgot everything.

. . . "Will he live?" the Eagle asked.

"He will live," Sara replied.

She straightened herself and folded her stethoscope. It was morning. The Japanese was still unconscious, but he was breathing normally since she had given him a transfusion at five o'clock. There had been a fuss about blood. No one had wanted to give a Japanese blood, though his type was ordinary enough. Suddenly, to everybody's surprise, Dr. Chung had come into the room.

"Take mine," he said.

"No!" It was Siu-mei's voice crying out. "No, I don't want—"

But Dr. Chung's face moved slightly in an ironical smile. "A little Chinese blood will do him good."

He was scarcely paler when Sara had drained off the blood, but he took the cup of broth Siu-mei had run to fetch for him, and together they had left the room. The Japanese man's heart had strengthened instantly.

"Then I will go back to the hills," the Eagle now said. "In seven days I will return to fetch him."

"It will be more than seven days before he can be moved," Sara said.

"How long?"

"Make it three times seven."

The young chieftain looked at her sternly. "But by that time I shall be pursuing the enemy far from here."

She smiled at his certainty. The Japanese armies were advancing upon the city, not retreating from it. The regular Chinese army had fallen back. Everybody was looking to the guerrillas for help. If the guerrillas failed, the city was lost, people were saying. The rich were already sending out their women and girls. At the Treaty

Port miles away by the river, American and English businessmen were sending away their wives and children in chartered airplanes. And here in her presence was the chief of the guerrillas!

"Why do you linger?" she asked. The Japanese lay unconscious between them. "You know the people look to you."

"Will you promise he will not die?" The chieftain's strong black eyes were upon her. "A handsome fellow," she thought irrelevantly, and wished Gray could see him. Gray so ardently admired these men of the hills.

"I cannot promise. I can only say he will not die," she replied.

"It is the best you can say?"

"The very best," she replied.

"You are honest," he said. For a moment something warm passed between them. He was a Chinese guerrilla, the son of Chinese peasant parents; she was the daughter of an American farmer, continents apart, oceans between; but they stood face to face, and she liked him and he liked her. She smiled.

"But if I keep him alive and return him to you, you must make me a promise," she said.

"Is it just to demand a promise from me when you will give none?" His voice was full of hearty humor.

"No, but this depends upon your own will," she replied, still smiling.

"I will give it to you," he said instantly. "What is it?"

"If I heal him, do not kill him."

He looked at her gravely and replied in a voice as grave, "I had no thought to kill him, if he lives."

"Why, then, should you keep him?" she asked.

"I told you, I have my own use for him," he replied, and turned and went away.

. . . The Japanese was conscious that same night. Sara went into his room when the first air-raid warning sounded, and he looked at her and saw her plainly, a white woman, English or American. He chose English out of the four foreign languages he knew. It was unusual for a Japanese to know so many foreign languages, but he had often wished in the last six months that he could exchange them all for Chinese. He understood not a word, not a sign, not a laugh of these Chinese; especially, never their laughter.

"What is that noise?" he asked faintly.

"We are about to have an air raid," she said, surprised at his English. This was indeed no ordinary Japanese. Was he, in spite of all she had said to the guerrilla, a sure-to-die?

"Have you—shelter?"

"Certainly," she said. "We have ample shelter."

God forgive her, she thought, it was not ample, but she would not tell a Japanese so!

"Then—move me!" The voice, so faint, was imperious.

"You are afraid of your own planes?"

"Assuredly. They are excellent marksmen."

"Yes," she agreed. "They hit the hospital regularly."

"Ah," the Japanese said, "I am sorry."

She saw to his moving and watched him wheeled away. Dr. Chung went with him. It happened that all the sure-to-dies this day were women—one of them a mother whose baby she had delivered an hour ago. She sent the baby away and sat down in the ward beside the unconscious mother.

She took no precautions nowadays. What did it matter if she died, except for these sick? She took the Chinese woman's narrow wrist between her finger and thumb. She was very young, too young to be a sure-to-die, a pretty child whose family were too poor to move away. If the baby had been a boy she would have sent to tell them it was born, but it was a girl and they would only have been angry to be roused out of bed for that. A girl dying for a girl—it was nothing for nothing, they would say.

The second warning sounded. By now the girl's family would be climbing the hills in that long patient line of working people who must stay in the city whatever befell. She thought anxiously that, if Gray came straight from the coast by plane, he might land at the port today. By plane he must come, since now the Japanese held the river, and the railroad in from the south was bombed daily. And he would, naturally, not risk—his wife. She quivered. If she had a moment between now and dark, she would pick some late chrysanthemums and put them in a bowl on the table in Gray's house. Lao Wang, the gardener, had already put flowering pots of them on the steps and veranda. If they did not come until tomorrow, the flowers would still be fresh enough. She had not been in the house since the guerrilla had found her there. She had never asked the Eagle further of his name, but when he was gone she asked Lao Wang. The common people knew all about guerrillas.

"Why is he called the Eagle?" she had asked.

"He is called the Black-browed Eagle because no one knows when he will dart down," the old man said. "He dwells in the hills, and from the skies he falls upon his enemy. As for his brows, they meet together upon his forehead."

It was true, they did. She remembered.

The bombs were falling again. One crash and she might be in a heap of ruins. The girl moved, and Sara took her hand and held it to quiet her. It was hot and dry and lifeless. She felt in her bag for a hypodermic, and while the earth shook and the air cracked and split she thrust it into the girl's arm. She was getting used to the bombs, so that now all that really seemed unendurable was the oppression upon her chest of the air rent and driven by the concussion.

Then there was a crash that silenced everything else. She cowered upon the bed and held herself in a knot, waiting. Surely the walls must fall! But they stayed. And after a moment she straightened herself. There was the familiar hiss and spit of the defending Chinese plane— only one this time, one solitary fighting plane darting and springing hither and thither. Was the girl dead? Yes—a moment's examination told her that this one life was over. The riven air had been death to her. What about the little baby, then? Perhaps the family would not want it in these times. Maybe she could keep it. Why not? One must have something.

She was glad the raid was early today. She glanced out of the window. The little house was quite safe. She could go and put chrysanthemums in it. Then she saw the gatehouse had been struck. The brick pillars were in piles, and the heavy wooden gates, bound in brass, were splintered. The hospital sign, that the magistrate of the city had once given them when his son's appendix had been taken out safely, was cracked in two. "House of Mercy," it had said in high black and gold letters. But now "Mercy" lay tossed aside.

"I'll have to get that mess cleared up," she thought. "If Gray should come, they can't get in."

But she had no time for it. The patients were coming back, in wheeled chairs and stretchers and leaning on nurses and orderlies; and the babies were screaming and hungry. It was the Japanese, though, who terrified her. He had gone unconscious again. Dr. Chung hurried at his side.

"I doubt . . ." he began.

32

"Take him in at once," she ordered. "Have you given him a stimulant?"

"All I dare."

"I'll try that new compound of mine," she said. She had been experimenting with special stimulants for shock. The ordinary ones were too often harmful to hearts fluttering into silence.

Two hours later she and Dr. Chung looked at each other over the gray face on the pillow.

"What is your opinion?" she asked.

"He is better than he was half an hour ago."

"I think so—and if he is, it is you must have the credit."

Dr. Chung shook his head. "Your X compound."

"But you administered it so exactly. I timed your doses—each had just the right effect. Very delicately done, doctor."

"Thank you, doctor."

She wanted to say that it was all the more admirable because this man was an enemy. The Chinese doctor's ethics were admirable, even if she did not like him. Modern medicine was new in this old country and modern medical ethics newer. But the thing was difficult to express, and as she was thinking of it she heard the popping of firecrackers and jumped. That could mean but one thing—Gray had come! For days Lao Wang and Siao Fah had had strings of firecrackers ready for the instant when Gray should appear.

She ran to the window and saw Gray climbing over

33

the debris of the fallen gate, a laughing Gray, looking, she saw instantly, brown and happy and strong—not the tired, white-faced man who had left in the summer heat of June. And he had his arm around a slender girl, a girl whose face she could not see under the brim of her hat. He held her while her dainty feet went slipping over the plaster and broken brick, and Lao Wang and Siao Fah stood side by side holding the long strings of popping firecrackers, and from all over the compound nurses and orderlies were running to welcome Thomison doctor and his bride.

She turned, to find Chung at her side. "Will you go down—or I?" she asked.

"You, of course—I will stay," he said.

She thought of her promise to the Eagle. No, it was not a promise, but a responsibility. She must not leave the Japanese alone with this Chinese. And yet, and yet, had he not saved the man's life? Twice he had saved the life of his enemy, once with his blood and now once more by his skill.

"I shall not be long," she said.

"Be as long as you like, doctor," he replied.

Under the suavity of his voice, behind the smooth gleam of his eyes, she discerned the laughter of his knowledge of her. She stiffened and refused to acknowledge anything that he knew.

"Thank you, doctor," she said, and she went down to meet Gray.

II

AT THE WIDE-FLUNG DOOR of the hospital she met him. She had forgotten how beautiful he was, his brown eyes, the sun on his brown head. He had a new suit—she saw everything at once—and even a new hat in his hand, and a red tie, the wine-red she loved. She cried out, "Oh, Gray!"

And then, as though she had looked into a mirror, she saw herself in a pair of cool amber eyes, very pretty eyes, black-lashed and wide. She began to stammer.

"I haven't—I'm filthy—we've just had an air raid—the mother of one of my babies died. I haven't had time to brush my hair or wash my face."

Gray laughed aloud. "Sara, you—you're just exactly the way I knew you'd be. Louise, this is Sara."

"How do you do," Louise said in a soft voice, pretty and clear, like her face.

"How do you do," Sara said. Then she turned to Gray. "Your house is all ready, except chrysanthemums. I'm sorry I can't go over with you—but there's a Japanese I ought to— But probably you'd rather go alone."

They were both staring at her now, Gray in laughing amazement at her.

"A Japanese?" he began.

But she did not hear him. She could not bear to see these two—either of them.

"Excuse me," she muttered.

She turned and left them standing there and fled up the stairs and to her own room. There, there Gray could never follow.

And Gray, lifting his American bride over the threshold of his Chinese house, felt a secret tender alarm. Louise was so slight, so exquisite. Could she endure his life? He kissed her gently before he let her down.

"Be happy in my home, my dear."

He did not notice her silence. On the veranda Siao Fah gaped at him. Gray laughed at his shocked gaze.

"It is our custom," he told Siao Fah. "For a man to lift his new wife over his doorstep brings luck to the house." The kiss he forebore to explain. Siao Fah could never comprehend that.

Then he shut the door and turned to Louise. She was sitting in his easy chair, smoking a cigarette, her hat still on her head.

"What were they saying at the gate—all those people?" she asked.

He threw himself on his knees beside her and took her hands. "They were wishing us good luck."

"What sort of luck?"

"Oh—all that Chinese consider luck—boy babies, peace, harmony—Siao Fah said he hoped my wife would be industrious and saving."

Gray laughed, and Louise smiled the smallest of her pretty smiles. He leaped to his feet and pulled her up with him. "I can't believe I'm here, where I'd rather be than anywhere else in the world!"

"Gray—why?"

He took off her hat so that he could see her face against his breast. "Why, darling? I can't tell you. Maybe because it is that everything a doctor does here counts. At home if somebody's sick he can go from one doctor to another. Here there's only me—and Sara, of course, for the women. Everything we do counts for hundreds of miles around. Every nurse we train and every Chinese doctor we teach is another oasis in a desert of suffering." His arms dropped. "God, how they can take suffering, these Chinese! I tell you, Louise, it just makes nothing of any little personal problems to see how these people have taken this bombing for two years. Think of it—two years of not knowing whether the next day you'd be alive or not, never knowing when you go to bed at night whether you can sleep an hour, two hours—die in your bed, maybe, and never wake at all—and they haven't any more idea of surrender today than they ever had—"

She stood pulling her gloves through her hands and watching him with her big amber eyes. They were

37

beautiful eyes, clear under her black brows and lashes, and she knew it.

"Gray!" His name spoken in that soft sharp fashion cut across his thoughts like a door slammed.

"What, sweetheart?"

Whenever she lifted her eyes like that to look at him because he was so much taller than she, his heart crumpled and quivered. He knew in his core that he was sentimental as he would have loathed sentimentality in anyone else. She made him want to cuddle her and talk baby talk and behave in a way that made even himself aghast. But she was so small, so dainty, such a little butterfly of a thing! He tried often to put into words what she was, and could never catch the right likeness to bird or flower that he felt in her. Now he put his arms around her gently, lest he hurt her. So he was not prepared for what she said.

"Why didn't you tell me Sara was beautiful?"

For a moment he did not know how to answer her. His thoughts had been so remote from Sara, so joyously full of himself and Louise, that instinctively he was first shocked and then angry.

"Louise, damn it—"

"Don't swear, please, Gray. I only asked a question."

"But, Louise, such a fool question!"

"I don't think so. This Sara of yours is quite—good-looking."

"Don't call her *my* Sara!"

38

"Well?"

She had pulled away and stood there, waiting. He felt as helpless as a bull with a ring in its nose and ~ enraged.

"Louise, I won't be asked such questions. Good God, I thought it was only in plays that women said such things!"

"Well, Gray?"

The ring jerked a little in his nose.

"Well, nothing! Why didn't I tell you Sara was pretty? Because I didn't think of it. I'm in love with you, my wife. I don't see that anybody else is pretty. I don't know it. I don't see them—don't care to see them."

"You must have seen Sara a good deal when you were alone here together."

"We never were alone! Louise, can't you understand that when two doctors are working in a hospital—" He saw her underlip begin to tremble and cursed himself. "Sweetheart, you're tired." He put his arm about her. "Come on and look at the house a minute, and then I'm going to put you to bed. Siao Fah will get some dinner. You haven't even spoken to Siao Fah yet."

He guided her gently from room to room. "Good old Sara—she's done the best she could for us. But there will be things you'll see to do. This is going to be your home, honey—everything's to be the way you want it."

She let herself be led, her core stiff and hard against all she saw, but she hid it. In the kitchen Siao Fah stood very

39

clean in a new blue apron. He had made up his mind instantly against his new mistress, and then determined that nothing would separate him from Gray—Gray, whom he loved, whose socks he wore and whose handkerchiefs he stole, and upon whose food he took a liberal squeeze, whom he defended from all others who would have preyed upon him, and for whom he would have died, cheerfully and willingly, if it would have done Gray any good to have a stubby, pock-marked Chinese cook-boy die for him. He made up his mind to ignore Gray's wife. So far as he was concerned, he and Gray were keeping house alone together in this nice new house.

"Do you want your eggs done just the same at breakfast?" he inquired gravely.

"Certainly," Gray replied. "Why do you ask?"

"I thought America might have changed you," Siao Fah replied.

"Not at all. But your mistress likes her eggs cooked only three minutes."

Siao Fah made no sign of hearing this.

Gray went on, "We will have our dinner in the bedroom. Your mistress is tired."

Siao Fah looked excited. What! So to begin with a new wife as to spoil her by feeding her in bed!

"It is bad luck," he said loudly.

"What bad luck?" Gray asked.

"To bring the first meal to—her—thus." The word "mistress" stuck in his throat.

Gray laughed. "Nonsense—this is her house now."

Siao Fah turned his back. It was true, then, what he had heard about American women. He groaned over a potato. "I shall not desert him," he thought devotedly. "I will protect him in his own house." Of the two pigeons he had bought for dinner he chose the larger one for Gray and stuffed it delicately. The small, scrawny one he finished without enthusiasm for Louise. When it was in the charcoal oven he remembered he had forgotten to salt it and was pleased.

In the bedroom Gray was taking off Louise's shoes and stockings. Then he unpacked her suitcase and found her froth of a nightgown. Her things were so lovely, so like herself. He buried his face in the soft stuff and was suffocated with its sweetness.

"Dearest—dearest," he muttered, "why me, out of all the world?"

. . . Louise, in the narrow bamboo bed, her soft light brown hair curling over the pillow, asked herself the same question. Why, out of all the world, must she love Gray? What had prompted her that Sunday morning in a Park Avenue church to fall perversely in love with the tall dark-eyed man who stood in the pulpit to tell them about his hospital in China?

41

She had been full of restless idle energy that morning. The season was just beginning again—her third New York season. The first had been so wildly exciting. She had been the chosen debutante that year, the one to symbolize all others. Her mother and father had laughed and been indignant, but secretly they had been pleased, though they pretended impatience at reporters and photographers and publicity. But her younger sister, Inez, had been abjectly worshipful. Poor Inez—her debut this year had been flat disappointment because she had been only a debutante. But then, Inez was only ordinarily pretty and she, Louise, had been, everybody said, extraordinarily so.

She was prettier now than then, too, but it did her no good—in a girl's third season nothing did much good. The flock of new girls kept pushing up from the bottom, and people only wondered, if you weren't going to have a Hollywood career, why you didn't get out of the way and get married. She had been engaged four times, the last three times secretly, after the public fuss over Timmie Woodall and his trying to kill himself because she had changed her mind. Well, how did she know beforehand that she was simply going to be tired of the way he wanted to kiss her all the time? When she told her mother this, her mother looked at her queerly. "Certainly you had better break it off if he makes you tired even before you are married," she had said.

So she had broken it off, as she had a perfect right to

do, and it would have been all right if Timmie hadn't been spectacular and a spoiled only child. Of course her family had been old friends with Timmie's, and both had money. But she couldn't help that. And one after the other, Jack and Lewis and Hartwen—without exactly knowing why, none of them—and there had accumulated in her that enormous nervous impatience. She ought to marry or else do something. But there was noth ing she wanted to do, and no one she wanted to marry, and she could not travel because Europe was a ferment, and where else could one go? She had grown mildly interested in Japan because she met some people in the Adirondacks who had been there, and they said it was really a wonderful country, neat and clean and ordered. The Japanese were wonderful organizers, like the Germans. Sometimes she wondered if She had had a wonderful summer, once, in Germany.

Gray came in from the bathroom rubbing his dark hair. "What are you thinking about?" he demanded. "You look like an angel, thinking heavenly thoughts."

"I was thinking of the first moment I saw you," she said, smiling.

"Tell me all over again," he demanded, sitting beside her.

"You're vain," she said. "You want me to say that I thought you the best-looking man I ever saw."

"Did you?"

"You know I did."

43

"Did you fall in love with me instantly?"

"Well, I thought maybe I could."

He took her hand and put it against his cheek.
"Louise, why didn't I know such a tremendous thing was
happening there in front of me? I should have stammered and stuttered and felt the earth trembling and the
heavens shaking. Instead I went on as coolly as anything,
asking for a million dollars for my new hospital and
thinking about nothing except getting it, by George!"

"I know—and I'm terribly hurt!"

He laughed and tousled her head on the pillow. "Well,
I got my million, thanks to your dad and mine com-
bined, and as soon as these Japs let up you're going to see
a real hospital, my girl, a hospital that New York
wouldn't despise."

"Gray, China and Japan are very different, aren't
they?"

He stared at her. "I'll say—about as different as—
as— Why, they're the most different two peoples in the
world. They think differently and live differently, they
believe in different ways of life. The Chinese are all for
the individual and the Japanese for the state—it's essen-
tial democracy and fascism—in a way."

"Sometimes I wonder if people ought to be so free. I
mean when they're ignorant and dirty."

She thought distastefully of the streets she had seen in
the disorder of Shanghai and of the medievalism of
Chen-li. It took only a few minutes to see what Chen-li

was, though Gray had told her that it was medieval. "You'll have to have your bath carried in wooden buckets and poured into a big porcelain jar, but you can get just as clean as in any other tub," he had said. But need people live in medievalism in a modern world? Maybe it was silly to live in Chen-li. Gray laughed.

"Don't you go giving up the idea of liberty and equality, my girl," he said. "That's poor business for a newly married woman."

She let him laugh, puzzled at her own mood. Why did she feel peevish and crisscross and like contradicting everything?

Suddenly she knew. Sara's clear voice cried out from the living room. "I've brought your chrysanthemums, everybody!"

"Come here!" Gray shouted, leaping to his feet. A second, and Sara stood in the door. She had taken off her uniform and put on a wine-red silk. She had brushed her hair, and her cheeks were flushed but her blue eyes were steady. In her arms she held an enormous bouquet of Chinese chrysanthemums, huge nodding balls of red and yellow and brown and orange.

And Louise, looking at her, felt her mood clarified and hardened and made as cold and changeless as a crystal shape.

"I'm going to hate everything," she thought, and made up her mind to it.

. . . "This is simply nonsense," Louise thought, in the shelter.

In the middle of the night she and Gray had been waked by hoarse screeching sirens. There had been no time to ask anything. Gray hustled her into her clothes, into her fur coat.

"The shelter's dripping damp," he said. "You may be there for hours."

She did not at that moment notice his "you." It did not occur to her that he would leave her. They hurried across the dying autumn grass into the hospital, and by then the siren was screaming again.

"God, they're in a hurry," Gray muttered. "Get along, dear. I ought to help at the hospital."

"I thought you said you weren't going to feel—responsible—until tomorrow," she panted. She had on her warm bedroom slippers, and she was not used to walking without heels.

"I know, but I haven't the gall to let Sara do it without me. She's had months of it while I've been sleeping every night."

She said no more. Was she going to have to keep hearing about Sara?

Down the ramps improvised over the old wooden stairs the stretchers were coming, and men and women hobbling and little children carried in nurses' arms.

"No use your going up with me," Gray said hastily. "Just keep with the crowd."

"Gray!" she cried. "You aren't going to leave me?" She had not dreamed that he would leave her. And he, he had not dreamed that she would think him free to go with her. The sight of her face swept away his impatience. Of course she would be afraid in her first air raid. But there was no time.

Gray, I won't go alone."

"Honey, you'll be with everybody—all these people."

"Gray, you must come with me!"

"Louise, I can't—I'm a *doctor!*"

The Chinese were looking at her strangely as they passed, the white woman clinging to the man. Gray was desperate.

"Listen, Louise, the last warning will sound at any instant. Then the planes will be here. You've got to be in shelter, do you hear? I'd never forgive myself if— Louise, listen to me!"

She dropped his arm. "Very well, Gray." Her voice went dead. She turned in cold obedience and joined the crowd of sick Chinese. She loathed them, she told herself. If she had known they were going to be like this, she would never have let Gray come back. There were wonderful opportunities for him at home—that invitation to come to Johns Hopkins for oriental diseases. Baltimore was an aristocratic old Southern town. Besides, sick people were the same anywhere, weren't they?

The third siren sounded and everybody ran—tried to run. She herself made haste and was among the first few

47

to enter the winding opening in the hillside behind the hospital. She drew back against the wall, to be away from the people crowding in.

Now, so unexpectedly that she jumped, she heard her name called in English.

"Mrs. Thomison?"

She looked into the handsome face of a young Chinese.

"Yes?"

The man bowed. "I beg your pardon. I would like to introduce myself, Dr. Chung. I am assisting Dr. Gray as house surgeon. I must apologize that I was not able to meet you. I could not leave my patient at the time." He motioned to a stretcher where a man lay with his eyes closed.

"I am glad to hear someone speak English," Louise said. "This is my first air raid, and I'm a little nervous, naturally, especially as my husband felt he must stay in the hospital."

Dr. Chung's smooth face did not change. "I am sorry he felt it necessary. I met him, as a matter of fact, and offered to stay for him on your account. But both Dr. Thomison and Dr. Durand have a strong sense of duty. It is admirable."

Then Sara, she thought, was there too!

The man on the stretcher opened his eyes. "Give me some water," he said distinctly and in English.

48

Dr. Chung opened a thermos and poured it out. The man drank and closed his eyes again.

"He speaks English too," Louise remarked.

"He is a Japanese," Dr. Chung replied. "A very interesting case, the captive of a guerrilla chieftain famous in this region. The chieftain brought him in. This Japanese speaks no Chinese, naturally—but his English is very good, for a Japanese."

The siren shrieked once more, and Dr. Chung's face changed. "Stoop," he cried. "Hang your head, open your mouth, cover your ears!" He did himself what he commanded her to do, and everybody cowered. Only the Japanese did nothing. He lay with his eyes closed.

They waited while the drone of the planes grew huge, filling the close air of the winding passage of the shelter. Louise, pressed upon by the people, felt her terror braced with anger. "Stupid, stupid," she was thinking. "It's too stupid for me to be here. I don't have to be here. I don't have anything to do with all this. I'm an American—I ought to be in America. I oughtn't to be in all this. I don't have to go through with it."

And all the time the whirring wings and roaring motors were diving downward, and then there began the explosions of bombs, one after the other, some near, some distant. The air grew scant. People lifted their heads to gasp. She lifted hers, driven for air, and saw the Japanese. His mouth was open and his face gray. She touched Dr. Chung's arm and pointed to him.

"Dead?" Her lips made the word, but her voice was soundless.

The doctor took a hypodermic from his pocket, but at his touch the Japanese opened his eyes and shook his head, and the doctor put it away.

She hung her head again. There was another explosion. She was angry with Gray. He had no right to bring her to this. He ought to have told her—not as he did tell her, just saying, "You're sure you won't mind the air raids, dearest? There isn't much danger of your getting hurt. I don't believe that even a direct hit would get the hospital shelter—Sara and I worked it out pretty well— passages instead of big spaces in the rocks so that crowds couldn't get hurt. And Sara had the idea of making the entrances crooked, so as to check the concussion, you know, and plenty of exits, so if one gets crashed in. You get used to it after a while when you realize that there is no danger."

But he had lied. She would never get used to this, never, never!

. . . When the din was over and the earth had ceased to tremble and the air stopped quivering at last, she lifted her head. She was so shaken that it was all she could do to keep from crying. But the people around her were moving quietly and getting up. Near her a child had gone unconscious, and a pretty Chinese nurse —no, a doctor—the nurses were in blue—was giving it a stimulant. The woman doctor turned and called to Dr. Chung, who went to her and bent over the child and examined its eyelids.

Louise leaned against the wet rock. Her chest hurt her, and her knees trembled. She put her hand to her hair and found it damp around her forehead. The silence was like a weight after the noise. It was hard to move her neck or lift her hand. She let her head drop on her breast, and met the wide-opened eyes of the Japanese, looking up at her.

"This is too much for you," he said distinctly.

"Yes, it is," she said through dry lips. Even her tongue was dry.

"Why are you here?" he inquired.

"My husband is the doctor," she replied.

"He should send you away," he remarked quietly. "To suffer unnecessarily, it is foolish."

Before she could answer, he had closed his eyes, and she felt she need not answer. Besides, what could she answer? He was right.

The siren sounded again for safety, and the waiting people came streaming out of the rocks. She went with them, dazed and trembling, into the darkness. Where was Gray? Even yet he did not come. Where was she to go? She did not even know the way to their house.

"May I help you?" Dr. Chung's voice came out of the darkness dimly lit by flashlights.

"I'm afraid I don't know my way yet," she stammered.

"Go with her," the Japanese was speaking from his stretcher. He had a flashlight, and he played it on the Chinese doctor. "Take her to her home."

She felt the light on her own face a moment, and saw the gray delicate lines of the Japanese face like a mask in the night. The eyes, which she now saw fully from the front, were bright and alive—not, she thought, astonished, the eyes of a sick man at all!

"Thank you," she faltered.

. . . Long after she was in bed again, shivering and solitary, Gray came in. It was so long she had had time for everything—time to weep, until her tears dried up in anger; time to be angry; time to grow cold in strong determination. When Gray came in she turned on her back and faced him as he stood at the foot of her bed. She had lain for an hour, hardening herself against tenderness from him, against his possible anger, against argument. She could be determined beyond any of that. Long ago her father and mother had come to dread that power in her to have her own way.

"Don't let Louise start her stubbornness," her mother would cry in a panic. She had let them beguile her out of it sometimes if they gave her enough in exchange. But there was nothing large enough that Gray could give in exchange for what she had been through.

"Gray," she said, "I've made up my mind. You've got to take me home."

But Gray offered no exchange, and she had not prepared herself enough for his calmness. He was neither
tender nor angry.

"Louise," he said, "I won't do it."

. . . His own words shocked him as they left his lips.
He had come back from the hours with Sara lifted into
exaltation. He had forgotten in the first happy weeks
of his marriage, in the peace and ease of his own country,
what it was to live through such hours as he and Sara
had just shared. The faces of the sick as they came down
the ramp in the hospital—when he saw them he wanted
Louise safe so he could forget her, forget even love, in
this larger thing which was his duty. He had turned
once when he was on the stairs and he saw her going
out of the door with the crowd. It was right. He and
she were at this moment only two in a host.

He went swiftly upstairs, speaking to all he knew and
to those he did not. But they still needed no comfort,
these people, he thought. They had accepted resistance
to an enemy as their life. An old man with an amputated
leg stumped past him on crutches. He was chattering to
a man whose skin was sulphur-yellow with malaria.

"What I say is, every time a bomb drops, it's hundreds
of Japanese dollars gone. What I say is, it doesn't cost
us anything if we hide in the earth. It can't go on forever,
this dropping of bombs!"

Gray smiled and went on to find Sara tucking babies

into the baby wagon. She was working quickly, humming under her breath as she always did when she was working against time.

"This is all pretty swell," Gray said. He wanted to tell her how wonderful it was to him to see the way those people—everybody—took the beastliness that threatened them. But he could not. The sight of her brave blue eyes and her flushed cheeks as she put one little creature after another into its place simply choked him. Besides, Siu-mei stood waiting. Sara did not answer.

"There," she said to Siu-mei, "now you can take them." She bent over one very small baby girl and kissed the tiny brown cheek. "That's mine," she said.

"Yours?" he repeated stupidly.

She waved Siu-mei on and watched the wagon being trundled down the corridor.

"Her mother died yesterday, and the family don't want her. They say they can't take care of her. So I will keep her."

"Sara, how can you with all else?"

"Siu-mei will help me. I wouldn't trust anybody else with all those babies except Siu-mei."

She thought of telling Gray that she was sure Siu-mei and Dr. Chung were falling in love with each other, and then decided she would not. It would be too hard to speak to Gray of any love. The second siren sounded.

"We had better look once more at the sure-to-dies," she said. "Amazing how often they don't die! I try to keep them together so that they won't realize that they are not being moved."

"Why does Chung leave this to you?" he asked.

"I sent him to the shelter today," she replied, and made up her mind after all that she would tell him about the young Chinese pair. "The truth is that he and Siu-mei—" She stopped in the middle of the corridor between the two hospitals. "Gray!" she cried. Her face was bright with horror.

"Why, what? Sara, what on earth!" He stared into her widening eyes.

"Gray, you oughtn't to be here! I've only just remembered—Louise!"

"Louise is all right," he said.

"No, but you, Gray—you can't stay here! What if—Gray, hurry, hurry! There's still time. Look, it'll be five or six minutes maybe before the planes come. Go on, Gray—go on, go on—"

"I won't go on!"

"You must think of Louise—you haven't the right."

"This is my job."

"But I don't want you here, Gray. I can manage. I've managed very well alone. And I haven't anybody to—to care as Louise does. Now look, Gray—"

He seized her arms. "Shut up, Sara. Shut up, shut up! You don't know Louise. She'd hate me if I were a shirker. She'd be the first to kick me out if I ran for cover."

"No, but, Gray, it's not necessary for you to be here. If it were necessary—"

He broke in. "What about you going into the shelter for a change? You've been going through this day after day, alone—"

"I'm—used to it."

"Used to nearly getting killed every day, eh? Well, you're just about used enough."

"Let me go, Gray." She was acutely conscious of his hands on her arms. But he did not release her.

"Will you obey me?" he demanded.

"No," she said quietly.

"Why?"

"Because I know what I must do."

He dropped his hands. "So do I, Sara."

"Very well, Gray."

They went on after that in silence, visiting the sure-to-dies. There were over thirty of them. The third warning sounded, and instantly the planes were swarming over the city. Gray felt the sweat start from his skin. His heart flew to Louise, but each time he put the thought of her away. She was safe. He would despise himself if he were not here. The planes were not too near yet for him to hear Sara's clear voice at his ear giving him details of one patient after another.

"This is a case of infected shrapnel wound. The abdominal wall was pierced, and we have been fighting peritonitis—unsuccessfully, I fear—feel her pulse."

He felt the rapid, irregular pulse.

Sara sighed. "Such a nice woman! She is the wife of a farmer. Sometimes the Japs just dump their bombs on any village they see and we have scores of these cases."

Then the planes diving down shut off her voice. She drew him to a doorway by a touch of her hand upon his elbow, and they stood there side by side. He felt the sweat pouring down his body. Nothing was clear in his mind. Even Louise's face was dim. There was just this noise to endure, this hideous, useless, crazy noise to be got through with, that he had forgotten about for months.

But she was thinking, "This I share with him. I cannot share love, but I can share danger and perhaps death. It may be that these are greater than love."

As if the deep passion of her thinking had reached out to him, he turned his head as she turned hers and their eyes met. He saw her faithful face clear in the instant, her beautiful, faithful face. Louise was right. Sara was beautiful. He had looked at her hundreds of times and not seen how beautiful. He had only been annoyed at first that he had been sent a young woman whose good looks were a responsibility, troublesome among a people too shrewd to believe that a man and woman, both young and handsome, could work together without attraction. He had been determined to prove that it could be done. And he had fallen in love with Louise, not with Sara. If Sara had been a man he would have put his arm about

57

her shoulder in good comradeship—we who are perhaps about to die! A bomb fell and burst. He put out his hand and grasped hers, but after the instant she drew it away again.

. . . When it was over he was suddenly hungering for Louise. He wanted to pour out on her the bravery of the hours, the people coming quietly back to their homes from the hills, to take up their work where they left it if they found their houses still standing, the sick returning to their beds, the nurses hastening silently from one to another, hot food being brought from the kitchens by the servants. Downstairs Sara and he were receiving the newly wounded, examining, treating, sending those who needed operations to be made ready. He operated on four men, one after the other. Once he thought, "I should have sent word to Louise." Then he thought, "No, she's a doctor's wife."

When he was finished, he went through the downstairs halls to Sara's office and found her putting down notes.

"Aren't you going to sleep?"

Dawn was breaking through the sky in long lines of silvery light.

"I am just going," she said. "Good night, Gray."

"Good night, Sara." He hesitated. She had been operating too. "Did you lose any?"

"No—mine will pull through, unless we have to move them too soon."

"I have one shaky enough to scare me—an old fellow. But game as anything. He said, when I asked him if he'd let me take out an iron splinter from his thigh, 'You are too courteous—the Japanese didn't ask me if they could put it in!' He went under the gas chuckling at himself."

She smiled. "That's the way they are."

He felt choked again. "Pretty swell, eh, Sara?"

"Pretty swell."

"Well, good night."

"Good night, Gray."

He walked across the dim lawn full of the energy of his admiration for courage and laughter and faithfulness, a grand folk, grand to live with, grand to die for—and went into his house. He wanted to share it all with Louise. He wanted to draw her into the glory with him.

"Louise!" he cried.

Siao Fah came out of the kitchen with a tray of tea and toast. He had been in the hospital shelter but not near his mistress. He had watched her steadily, aware that she did not know his face among the others. Why did she talk with the Japanese? Why did the Chung doctor, whom nobody liked, bring her home when her husband was not there?

"That one is in her bed," he said to Gray. His face was empty. He put the tray down. "Eat something," he commanded. Then he turned and went back into the

59

kitchen. If she had been a proper wife she would have been up and waiting for her husband, and she would have seen that he had food. As it was, there was only he himself to look after the white doctor.

But Gray had gone straight to the bedroom and flung open the door. There she lay, lovely upon the pillows. She was awake, waiting for him, his wife. "Sweetheart!" he cried, his high heart rushing out to her.

And then had come those words of hers. And his own words of blunt refusal tore themselves out of him.

Because he couldn't! But how make her see?

Over her little face, pale upon the pillow, there came a cold prettiness. Her small perfect features sharpened, and her lips folded together into pure stillness. He had never seen so strange a look, and to his own astonishment he was terrified.

He flung himself on the bed beside her. "Sweetheart, don't look at me like that!"

She did not answer. She kept on looking at him steadily, two shafts of cool amber light falling upon him from between her lashes.

"Darling, say something—don't just lie looking at me!"

Her lips made the slightest movement. "I want to go home."

The words were almost soundless, but he heard them. "But, dearest, you haven't tried it here—not really. You'll get used to the raids. Look—everybody gets used to it.

Look at the sick people, even. God, they were wonderful! Getting out of their beds and hanging on somehow; and, darling, did you see the lights going up the mountain? They were—"

"I want to go home." She turned her head away. Her lips quivered and her eyelids fell.

"Oh, my darling, don't cry!" He gathered her in his arms, and she began to sob helplessly. "Louise—Louise," he moaned.

At the keyhole of the bedroom door, Siao Fah gnashed his teeth. Crying, was she? He listened hopefully for the sounds of a woman being beaten. But no, there were only the pleading, muttering noises a man makes when he is afraid of a woman. He tiptoed away and sat down in the kitchen and held his head in his hands and groaned and thought about poison, nothing to kill anybody, but a little powder put in soup, that would cause a mild illness or something, if severe, yet short of death. He did not want to kill anyone, even for Thomison doctor's sake. Then he gave it up. No, his master was a doctor who could cure anything. What did she want? Jewels, probably, fine clothes, the things women cried for! He thought with pleasure of his own wife, whom he kept soundly under his will with a bamboo switch. He had made a fine wife out of her.

In the bedroom Louise wept until she was filled with fatigue. It was not unpleasant, this weeping in Gray's strong arms. She was overwrought with the horrible night, and she wept away her strain, conscious of his arms beneath her. The fatigue was sweet, too, in its way. She felt helpless and little and clinging. Slowly she stopped weeping. Her sobs grew soft and infrequent. At last she lay silent, crumpled as a child. Gray had not spoken for a long time. She looked up at him, her lashes drenched and black.

"I do love you, Gray." Her voice was a baby's whisper.

He held her to him with a tenderness that terrified him. Why was he so afraid now in this quiet room, under the silent skies?

"I love you, my wife."

Her lids drooped, and she put her face in his breast. When she whispered again, her words seemed to come out of his own heart.

"Gray, then take me home!"

He groaned and held her closer, and answered as steadily as ever, "No, Louise."

III

AM I RECOVERING?"

Yasuda, who had gone through the Chinese doctor's examination without a word of speech, now asked this question. His voice was calm and without weakness.

"You are," Chung replied.

"If my captor comes today, am I well enough to be returned to him?"

"In my judgment, yes," Chung replied.

The two men spoke in English and equally well, and yet upon their tongues the language could have passed for two, had English been unfamiliar to the listening ear. The Japanese spoke with the guttural intonation of the German-taught. The Chinese had learned from an English missionary, educated in Oxford. But there was no one in the room to hear them.

Chung straightened himself and covered his patient. He began to put away his stethoscope, his delicate supple hands moving without a fumble. He had purposely come into this room alone, without the usual nurse. One of the nurses, Ya-ching, had been lingering near him, waiting to be called, but he had not noticed her. Half the nurses in the hospital were in love with him, he thought scornfully, and why should he pay Ya-ching any heed? She was pale and pock-marked. Why pay any nurse heed when Siu-mei was beginning to yield? Siu-mei's family was rich.

"Why do you work when you need not?" he had asked her one day.

"I wish to work," she had replied with a proud look. He himself worked because he desperately wanted money. His family were poverty-stricken, his father an idle son of a silk merchant who had used up the last of his small inheritance and, as if that were not enough, had now begun to smoke opium because of kidney pains. The large family of his younger brothers and his parents hung upon Chung with an intolerable burden. He was compelled by tradition to take the burden, but the years abroad had destroyed all feeling for his family. One missionary scholarship after another had paid for his education until his own brilliance had won him all he needed. He was quite willing to fall in love with Siu-mei, indeed, was more than half in love with her, but still the thing must not be brought too quickly to the point of money in his hand. She was sensitively romantic, and her newly budding love might shrivel if he spoke too soon of his need, and her family was old and conservative in the city, and a betrothal, even in the modern fashion, could not proceed too quickly. But he needed money now, at once. His father had sent his second brother this morning for more money. But Chung had already used his month's salary and had borrowed another, and he could not ask at the office for more.

"You seem to think that because the hospital feeds me and shelters me I do not need anything else," he had said to his brother.

"What more do you need?" the boy inquired innocently, food and shelter being all he strove for.

"I have a position," Chung said haughtily. "I am a Western-educated man with many degrees. I have my friends to consider. It shames me to be so poverty-stricken that I cannot give them a feast when it is my turn or pay my share of a little pleasure."

It was true that he had a small circle of ten or eleven men, educated abroad like himself, who clung to each other and looked up to him. They lived in the old Chinese city, alien and contemptuous of it. They discussed bitterly, though always in secret, the filth and poverty and helplessness of their own people, though they had loudly denied these things before white men in foreign countries. In secret, behind the closed doors of a room in a restaurant, they even told each other that it might be better if the Japanese took China under their control and made a modern nation of the huge shambling old country.

"Then afterward we could take it back again," they said, and felt themselves patriots.

Still, they enjoyed certain ancient vices, as, for instance, the pretty courtesans they hired for a night's feast, one to stand behind each man's chair. At such times how could Chung say that he had no money? Was he alone to endure the shame for having no one to stand behind his chair, and for so mean a cause as poverty? Unfortunately, in order to add to their respect for him as a leader among them, he had told his fellows that his salary was three times as large as it was, though it was good enough. As for giving up their amusements, all the young men would have felt it impossible. In these miserable times, when death threatened them daily, a few hours of amusement was all that made their life endurable.

So, therefore, though he had no definite purpose when he came alone this morning into the room where the Japanese lay, nevertheless certain thoughts had come into his anxious mind. This Japanese had money, even though he was a captive. He wrote checks weekly on a Shanghai bank, now in Japanese control.

"It is necessary for me to remain in the hospital," Yasuda said.

Chung was surprised, but he did not at once answer. He had been prepared to hear that Yasuda might wish to be helped down the river to a point where the Japanese army might find him.

66

"The hospital can scarcely keep one of its rooms needlessly occupied in such times, I fear," Chung said. His voice was entirely colorless. He went on rearranging and rearranging his stethoscope parts while Yasuda considered this.

"Your hospital needs money, doubtless, for its good work."

"No," Chung replied in the same colorless voice, "no, we are fortunate. Doctor Thomison's father is a very rich man. And I hear that Doctor Thomison's wife is also of a rich American family."

So sure was the touch of his hands that there had not been the clink of one metal part against another. Now he closed his bag swiftly and turned to his patient.

"I congratulate you on being so nearly well, Mr. Yasuda. Today there is no reason why you cannot get up for a little while, especially if we have no raids, and go out into the sunshine."

"I have no wish to get up," Yasuda replied.

Chung sat down. "This is strange," he remarked softly. He glanced at the door, and Yasuda caught his glance.

"Lock the door," he said.

Chung obeyed noiselessly.

"You are no ordinary man," Yasuda said abruptly.

Chung inclined his handsome head.

"Therefore I will speak to you frankly, as one intelligent man to another."

Chung did not answer. He lifted his head and gazed

at Yasuda's knobby, strongly-lined face with the calm and innocent gaze of a Buddha.

"We Japanese and Chinese do not hate each other," Yasuda went on. "There is no reason why we should not be friends, in spite of this war, which I myself deplore."

"I also," Chung murmured.

"Myself, I advised against it," Yasuda said. "At the time when the matter was discussed, though I am a high officer in the Japanese army, I said, 'It is foolish to attack the Chinese when we should make them our allies against the white man.'"

"How wise!" Chung agreed.

"You hate white men?" Yasuda inquired with energy.

"Entirely," Chung said. Did he not hate the white-faced missionaries who had heaped favors upon him and then reproached him because he despised their religion? Would he ever forgive the reluctance he felt in American girls when he asked them to dance with him? Where among those raw and uncouth college boys had there been one who was his equal? And yet the most uncouth could find his partner and he could not, fastidiously as he took care to appear at his best. He had come back from America sore with many small slights. The clamor of admiration in America for his country did not deceive him. The Americans considered themselves superior to him, putting him only a little above the black men they had brought from African jungles to be their slaves—he, the son of a civilization four thousand years old! When he remembered all this, he said with more violence than he had yet spoken:

"I do hate them, indeed."

"Good," Yasuda said. "Then you will agree with me when I say that it is the common task of Japanese and Chinese to drive the white man out of Asia."

"Entirely," Chung agreed solemnly. About this he could even feel patriotic. This hospital, for instance— If all white people were compelled to leave, he, a Chinese, would be its head. He began to see the usefulness of the Japanese. Alone, China could scarcely hope to drive out the white man. But if Japan drove them out, in the name of the conqueror of China, the difficult deed would be done. It would then only remain for the Chinese to drive out the Japanese, and there would be left China, their own country. It seemed easy and simple and clear. Anything which led to this conclusion would be his duty to do.

"Japan regrets this war, of course," Yasuda said. "But she has no choice now except to go on. To withdraw without victory would be unbearable. Our people would be disgraced before the world. Our honor is concerned."

"Certainly," Chung murmured.

Through the mists of pompous talk the two men began to discern each other. Yasuda cleared his throat.

"In short," he said, "if I could stay here, at a price decided upon, say, by someone in authority, like your-

69

self, I could hasten the fulfillment of our common purpose. For instance, the guerrillas into whose hands I mistakenly fell. They are very annoying to our advancing armies. If we knew, say, when they were planning to attack, it would greatly facilitate matters."

"It would be difficult," Chung murmured. But his mind was ranging over his large family of useless brothers, all idle, all wanting money from him. His second brother was a simple, good fellow, but the third one was clever and quick and a gambler who already knew how to win when he threw dice in the tea shops, as he did from morning to night. It would not be difficult to disguise him as a wandering soldier, deserter perhaps from the regular army, and so go to join the guerrillas. The boy had bold, honest-looking eyes, and if he were asked why he had run away from the army he could say, "Because they are retreating from the enemy, and I will not retreat." That would be a sure road to the Eagle's heart. After that the boy could come and go as he liked in the irregular spying of a guerrilla. That much was easy.

"There are many impossibilities," Chung went on in his calm ordinary voice, the English enunciation soft and pleasant to the ear. "For instance, even if you knew what you wish, how could you transmit it to your own men? The borders are carefully watched, the post office censored. No, communication is impossible—that is, regular communication."

Both men fell silent. Yasuda spoke first.

"Is the white woman doctor also rich?"

"No," Chung said. "But—" He shrugged his shoulders.

"Ah, a single-minded woman," Yasuda said. "I admire them, of course, but they are often in the way."

"What were you about to propose?" Chung asked.

"Merely that she might be willing to write an occasional letter to a certain post office in occupied territory—an innocent letter, but containing certain specified words. To tell all the truth, I am prepared with a code already, possible for use in several foreign languages. It is part of our foresightedness. Knowing the great prestige and power of the white man in your country, we foresaw that there might be times when we might need to use, say, an English code, in order to gain at least the respect of censors. This code may be expressed in business letters, in the letters of a pupil to an old teacher, of two friends, or even of two lovers. Love letters would perhaps be the least suspicious between two white people. White men and women are always writing love letters to each other, or so I am told."

"I do not doubt it," Chung agreed politely.

"But it is a pity we have only these two white people, one rich and so beyond temptation, one single-minded and so without imagination," Yasuda said and sighed. "Otherwise it would be simple. For instance, I am sure that my colleagues are daily expecting such a letter from me. We have in our employ a young white Russian, who

71

speaks all the necessary languages, whose sole duty it is to appear as a white man of a name already arranged, Henry Brown, and receive any letters I may send, under whatever name."

"Can you not pretend a name?" Chung asked.

"You know yourself I cannot in so small a place as this," Yasuda returned. "Your post-office officials are too shrewd. They know every white person in the town. No, it must be a letter from a known person, whose servant, bringing the letter among others, would be unquestioned."

"I fear it is impossible," Chung said, rising. His mind was in a ferment of excitement.

"It is too bad," Yasuda said. "I would ave paid a very large sum monthly to such a person."

"How much?"

"Half as much in a month as you earn in a year."

Chung's heart leaped like a fish in a pool. Thus might all his troubles cease!

"It is unfortunate there is no one," he said.

"I will increase it—as much in a single month as you earn in a year."

Before the steady gaze of Yasuda's deep-set eyes Chung's own handsome eyes flickered.

"I will return this afternoon for further examination, Mr. Yasuda," he said. "That is," he added, "unless we are raided."

"I forgot," Yasuda said. "If the letter is sent I can

promise one more thing—that the hospital will not be raided as long as I am in it."

Chung looked at him for a long moment. "Personally, as a Chinese, I am not afraid," he remarked, "but it may be—there are others unlike me."

He shut the door and walked quietly down the hall to his office, under his calmness astounded by the good fortune which might be his—which must be his, he thought in agitation—which would solve his every difficulty and raise him instantly to any place he wished among his fellows, relieve him of his family and give him time to marry Siu-mei. He was restless with excitement, and in his office touched a bell. A Chinese coolie in a clean blue hospital coat came in.

"Ask Dr. Siu-mei Ling to spare me a few moments," he said. "Tell her I wish to consult her about some X-ray photographs."

"So!" the coolie cried in customary assent and dog-trotted off.

In his office Chung could not sit still. Now might be the time for him to make his formal proposal to Siu-mei. They were modern, he and she, and there need be no nonsense of an old-fashioned go-between for them. He would ask her himself, he would tell her he had chosen her, and then they would inform the parents. The parents could be as old-fashioned as they liked, if he and Siu-mei understood each other. First to make sure of Siu-mei, and then he would proceed to the possibility

73

shaping in his mind, an enormous possibility, but it was shaping into the form of a small pretty American woman, whose terror had moved him to contempt. He had not told Yasuda of Louise Thomison. But he had thought of her instantly. She could be tempted.

The door opened, and Siu-mei came in.

"You sent for me?" she asked. Under her pale golden skin a deep rose color crept up from the high collar of her long Chinese robe of dark-green brocade. She was dressed to go out. She was off duty for the afternoon, and the messenger coolie had caught her as she was leaving her room next to Sara's. Her beauty and his own excitement made Chung hot, and a faint sweat broke out on his smooth upper lip.

"I wanted to show you these X-rays," he said. He picked up the photographs from his desk. Then he flung them down again. "Why do I pretend? I sent for you for one purpose."

Often enough he had seen upon American picture screens the approach of man and woman as lovers. But something in her kept him from that approach, the lovely dignity of a Chinese woman. He stood before her, not touching her.

"I wish to ask you—to invite you—to be my wife."

Her pretty face was all a rose now, but her eyes were brave.

"I—I thank you," she said, "but I—my family—I must speak with my father."

74

He interrupted her, "Naturally, but tell me first if you yourself can so consider me. You and I are what are called 'new' people. We are modern. Let us decide for ourselves."

She longed to say to him at once that she loved him. She knew she loved him, but she could not speak. The reserve of generations of separation between men and women still made a wall around her. She could not break it down alone to step outside. And he did not help her enough. The handsome face that she had come to look upon as the ideal face of a man, now that it was near, was suddenly remote in the very changelessness of its bland beauty. Her love shrank back.

"Let me think of it for a day," she said. "Let me tell you tomorrow."

His eyes flickered. "Tonight," he said. "Come, let us compromise. The night is hours away. I shall not sleep if you leave me uncertain."

Her heart yielded to his smile. "Tonight, then," she promised, and shut the door between them quickly.

And he, left alone, rubbed his soft supple hands together. Then he looked at his watch. It was nearly three o'clock. Dr. Thomison would most certainly not be at home at this hour. His wife would be alone. He went to a mirror that hung on the wall of his office and examined his face, smiled, and looked grave. He took a small bright green comb out of his pocket and parted his hair freshly and combed it down smoothly and straightened his collar. Then he strolled out of the hospital door into the still sunshine of the autumn afternoon and sauntered toward the bungalow, stopping once or twice to admire a particularly fine chrysanthemum in the flower border that ran along the bottom of the compound wall. He glanced at the sky. For once he would not mind an air raid. An air raid might help him. Since it had not come this morning, it was quite likely to come this afternoon. It would be a pleasant thing if in a raid the hospital could be an island of peace.

"A noble thing," he murmured, "very fine for the patients."

He went lightly up the stone steps of Gray's house and knocked at the door.

. . . Siu-mei, swaying gracefully in her riksha to the curve of the cobbled street, gazed about her. Once a week, on her day off duty at the hospital, she passed along this street and each time it looked different. Certain homes and shops were gone each time, but others were being built, some solidly of brick again as though the war were over, some of makeshift mats and bamboos. This week the changes were greater than ever. The raiding had been heavy. She was lucky to be going home instead of spending hours in the shelter. If she had had to take her secret into that long dim quiet today, she could not have borne it. She wanted to get out into air and sunshine. She wanted above all to talk with her father.

"Every seven days Chen-li is a new city," she said to her riksha coolie. She knew him well. For years he had kept his riksha at the stand in front of the hospital.

He laughed and wiped his face on the end of the strip of blue cotton cloth that hung over his shoulder.

"Yes, but the city is still here," he answered. "Our children and our grandchildren are still being born."

"Are you lucky?" she inquired.

"I had a grandson yesterday," he replied, as though he had given birth to it himself.

"And you did not send your daughter-in-law to the hospital to have the child properly born!" Siu-mei cried at him.

The old coolie did not stop trotting. He flung another laugh over his shoulder. "That son's wife of mine—she drops them like eggs!" he shouted.

They both laughed at that, and by now they were at the end of the long street, and he let down the shafts of the riksha with a flourish between two stone lions on either side of the big black wooden gate studded with heavy brass nails set in a pattern upon its two leaves. It was the gate of her father's house. Siu-mei stepped down and paid him and added the copper coins he expected.

"Bring your grandson to the hospital to show us, at least," she said.

"When his month is full," the man promised.

She nodded, smiled, and then pushed open the gate. Nowhere in the world did she feel the peace and security she felt always when she stepped into these courts. Even the war had not disturbed them. By chance the huge house of many courtyards lay at the foot of a hill, and her father had built a deep shelter far into the bowels of it. He had lined it with brick and furnished it comfortably and bought a foreign oil stove to burn against dampness. Here the whole enormous family of sons and daughters and their wives and children and the servants went always at the instant when the last air warning sounded. Food was lifted from the table if it were mealtime, beds were ready if it were night. There were children in this home who took as a part of life the daily shift to the shelter, not connecting it even with danger.

A servant saw Siu-mei and cried, "Shall I tell the mistress of your coming, little mistress?"

"No," Siu-mei replied, "I will go myself to my parents. Where are they?"

"In their own court," the servant replied. But she hurried off for fresh tea.

Through three courtyards Siu-mei walked, nodding here and there to someone working. It was very quiet. Her family was sleeping after last night's long raid. Well, if her father was sleeping he must wake at what she had to tell.

She stepped over the high threshold of a round gate

and into her parents' own living place. It was very still. The afternoon sunshine drifted down through bamboo upon the square tiles of the court. In the corner, beds of chrysanthemums blazed and a pool, shaped like a flower, was set in the middle of it. The water was blue under the sky and shot with the flashing gold of small fish. She crossed the court and entered the main room that opened upon it. Her father lay in a long bamboo chair, reading, his white beard on his bosom.

"Father," she said gently, not to startle him.

"Eh!" He looked up and put down his book. "You are late."

"I was delayed a few moments at the hospital." She sat down on the edge of a chair. She greatly loved her father. When she was three years old, at a time when girls' feet were still being bound, he had not allowed his old-fashioned mother to bind hers, and at a time when it was considered strange to educate girls he had sent her to school with her brothers. He was a man independent of his times. She was glad now she had found him alone.

"Where is my mother?" she asked.

"She is asleep, but she wished to be waked when you came in." He was about to clap his hands for a servant when she stopped him.

"No, wait, father. I had rather speak to you alone. Father, you have always said you wanted me to please myself, and yet that you hoped it would please me to be a man's wife."

"Yes, I have," her father replied. "Men and women are best when they are married to each other."

"But you have never chosen me a husband."

"No, because it is one of the good things about the new times that the young may choose each other and lift this responsibility from the old. My parents agitated themselves for years over choosing your mother for me. Before they decided they asked each other continually, was she the right one for me? After she was my wife they continued to agitate themselves asking, now that it was too late, whether they had done well and looking with long wishes at other young women. It was I who said, 'Comfort yourselves. This one is as good as any other, and for all I shall ever know, better.'"

His beard wagged mildly while he spoke, and his small dark eyes sparkled. She laughed. Her parents loved each other well, and all the house knew it.

"I have chosen, father," she said.

He looked instantly alarmed and sat up. "No, now, if you have chosen, that may be another matter!"

"Now, father, you cannot change your principles!"

"But what if I don't like him?"

"You will like him—he is intelligent!"

"Good." He stroked his beard quickly.

"And handsome."

"Good—good—that is very important in a husband."

"Well educated."

"Good, too, since you are educated."

"He earns money."

"Very excellent."

"He is modern."

"Necessary, for you."

"He is perfect."

"Ah, that is serious!"

"Why, father?"

"It means you can no longer see him as he is."

She examined him to see if he were joking, but his long mild face was grave. He pulled at his beard again.

"I suppose we must enter into formalities. But I had better know the name."

"He is the doctor at the hospital."

"You mean Chung Ming-liang?"

"Yes—do you know him?"

"I have heard of him."

"Only good, father!"

He did not answer at once. When he did it was a question. "How old is he?"

"Thirty-one, perhaps."

"Not a child."

"Nor am I."

"No."

He paused. "Personally, I believe in younger marriages. The man has no time for pastimes."

"We'll never be younger, father."

"That's true."

And then, as so often it seemed to happen, at this moment when she least wanted interruption the warning sounded for an air raid. Her father rose quickly and put all else aside.

"I must go to your mother. She will have waked too suddenly."

Within half an hour they were all gathered in the shelter, safe and comfortable; but there was the chatter and play of children, the bustle of servants, the exchange of family conversation, and then the roar of bombs. She and her father could talk no more.

. . . In the Thomison house nothing could have been more opportune than the warning of this air raid. Mr. Yasuda himself could not have been more helpful had he ordered it.

When Dr. Chung entered and asked for Mrs. Thomison, the sullen-faced Siao Fah pointed to the living room.

"I will tell her," he said.

He was a long time about it because he first went into the kitchen and considered whether he would tell her or would go point-blank to Thomison doctor and ask him to come home. He decided he would tell her. Give her space to stumble over the cliff, he thought, leave her time in which to show what she was! So he went and knocked on the bedroom door. The moment Thomison doctor left the house in the morning she went into that room and locked the door. He had to get it cleaned as he could while they were at breakfast. Now he heard the lock scrape. She stood there, clasping a long robe about her, her hair tumbled, her eyes red with crying. Since she spoke no language he could understand, he jerked his thumb toward the living room and made signs at her hair and robe.

"Dress yourself," he said distinctly in Chinese.

She did not understand. She peered into the living room. Then she called out and went back into the bedroom. He returned to his kitchen and drew a small three-legged stool up to the door. From experience he knew that when he sat on this stool his eyes were at the exact level of the keyhole.

"I'll be out in a moment," Louise had called. Why, she wondered, did this young Chinese want to see her? She disliked all Chinese, but he was a little more like an American. At least his English was perfect. She had not dressed herself properly for days. Why should she? There was nowhere to go. In the morning she put on a negligee, and when Gray was gone she went back to her bedroom to sleep and write long letters home to everyone she knew, to read something she had taken out of Gray's shelves. She had already finished the novels but, after opening one book after another of solid pages, she was beginning to read the novels over again. At night she put on one of her housecoats. Gray was easily deceived.

"You look gorgeous, sweet—what's this?" he asked, fingering velvet or silk or taffeta.

"Something I thought you might like," she said.

And day after day all the time she was tense with listening for the shriek of the siren that meant she must throw on her coat and rush to join the hobbling crowd of sick whom she feared and loathed. What were their filthy diseases? She shrank away from them. She drew toward the gentlemanly-looking Japanese with whom was always the handsome Chinese doctor.

"I thought Japanese and Chinese were supposed to be enemies," she had said once to Gray.

"So they are," he replied.

"That Dr. Chung seems friendly to that Japanese."

"He is too good a doctor to allow his personal feelings to influence him toward a patient," Gray had answered. "That Japanese, by the way, is about well enough to go back to the guerrillas who captured him."

"Won't they kill him?" she asked.

"Sara says not," he replied.

She let him mention Sara now without a word. She knew Sara was in love with him, but most of the time she could feel complacent. Gray did not know about Sara—he was too much in love with his wife.

She dressed herself now rather carefully in a thin dark blue wool with a wide white collar and went into the room where her visitor waited. Then she put out her soft, narrow little hand.

84

"How do you do," she said gently. She said it timidly, scarcely aware of her wish to please even a Chinese man.

He looked down into her pretty face. She was very young, he thought, and very pretty, prettier, even, than Siu-mei. The old hurt that American girls like this had once dealt him came alive. If he had been in her country she would perhaps not have put out her hand. He disliked intensely shaking hands with a man, but this little hand was pleasant.

Louise drew her hand away. His hand was very warm, and the palm was damp. His grasp was at once soft and powerfully strong. She felt a little afraid of him.

"Will you sit down? My husband—"

"I know your husband is not in, Mrs. Thomison. I came to see you—on a private matter."

"Yes?" Her eyebrows lifted slightly.

He leaned toward her, and she smelled a faint perfume. He was immaculately clean, and his American clothes made him seem not quite Chinese.

"Mrs. Thomison, I will be frank with you if I may be sure I can speak to you in confidence—in absolute confidence."

"You mean—not tell my husband?"

At the keyhole Siao Fah's small black eyes noted the lean of the man's body, the startled interest on the woman's face.

"Now he says something to her in that foreign tongue which he should not," he thought with great satisfaction.

"I cannot speak otherwise," Chung said.

Louise drew back. Was this the oriental intrigue which she had seen in so many stories and pictures? She began to stammer.

"I don't think—I couldn't, I'm afraid."

"It will save many lives," he said, "many, many lives." This, he saw at once, was the wrong thing. Her face did not soften.

"You are so frightened," he said gently. He had a voice that he could shape to the tones of music. "This life is too hard for you."

Ah, now he was right. Her lips quivered. He went on: "Let us forget what I came to say, Mrs. Thomison. Do you know you are not looking well? You stay in the house too much, but who can blame you?"

At the keyhole Siao Fah pursed his underlip. Ah, if only he understood English! And yet who needed to understand the words between a man and a woman who looked like this?

"I— It's just I'm not used to—to—everything," Louise said faintly. This morning in a letter to her mother she had said, "The only real understanding word I have had has been from a Japanese—of course, I can't say such a thing even to Gray, but the truth is I think I'd like them."

"Of course not," Chung said pityingly. "I have lived for years in America. I know everything that shocks you— the poverty, the dirty streets, the lack of ordinary conveniences in your home, the beggars."

"It is wonderful of you to understand," Louise murmured gratefully.

"I do understand—and I do not blame. And on top of all else, these fearful raids! But they at least could be prevented—at least your life could be safe," Chung said earnestly.

"How?" She was not afraid of him now.

"This Japanese gentleman in the hospital—Mr. Yasuda —if he could get word through to the Japanese army that he was here, their planes would not bomb the hospital. Of course, they do not know he is here."

"Then—why doesn't he just tell them, a telegram or something?"

"Our censorship is very strict," Dr. Chung said. "Every telegram, every letter to the enemy is blocked. But you could help, Mrs. Thomison."

"How could I?"

"If your name were signed to a letter, a short ordinary letter about something else, an American name, and Dr. Thomison is very well known here. Of course I do not ask you to sign his name—only your own. It might be you would have to sign a letter or two every week, merely to let them know Mr. Yasuda is still here. Then the hospital would be safe—your husband, yourself—"

He watched her closely.

"But why shouldn't my husband do it?" she asked.

Chung shook his head. "Dr. Thomison is so generous toward my people. He hates all Japanese. But we know, you and I, that not all Japanese are evil, even if they are our enemies. Mr. Yasuda is a gentleman and a kind man."

She did not answer at once. She knew he was right. Never, never would Gray ask a Japanese for protection. Once, when she had dared to say that the Japanese were cleaner than the Chinese, he had been furious.

"I'd rather have a man's skin dirty than his heart," he had replied.

She had said nothing. There were many things about which she could say nothing to Gray—more and more, as they went on living together.

She lifted her head. "But the letters wouldn't—incriminate me, would they?"

He laughed. "Not in the least! You shall read them—friendly letters, between a woman and her friend—a friend, say, called Henry—Henry Brown."

She looked relieved. "You mean I wouldn't have to write to a Japanese?"

He shook his head and smiled. "No, indeed—to a European!"

And, as if the Japanese came to help him, there sounded the warning of the approaching air raid.

"Ah," he said, "here they come—shall it be, perhaps, for the last time?"

They rose together, and she went into the bedroom to put on her coat. Through the keyhole Siao Fah watched intently. Chung doctor was smiling—men smiled when they were able to deceive women. Louise came back with her coat. The second warning sounded.

"They are in a hurry today," Chung remarked. "It's not a good sign. The raid will be severe. Let us go."

He took the coat from her and held it, and she slipped her arms into it. Then she paused to turn her head to look at him.

"Let me think it over?" she begged him.

"As long as you like," he said. Nothing, he thought, could have been luckier than this raid.

Siao Fah, not moving, saw her upturned face and the man's answering smile. He watched them go out of the door together before he himself locked the kitchen door to saunter toward the shelter. The only question now remaining in his mind was, when would he tell Thomison doctor of what he had seen? Tonight? Tomorrow? The knowledge was like a secret weapon. Not tonight, not tomorrow.

"I will keep it," he thought, "until I need it most."

IV

THE RAID was over again. Gray looked at Sara haggardly over the dead body of Lao Wang on the operating table. The old man had delayed too long in his garden. Sara looked back at Gray sadly. He turned away abruptly and, stripping off his rubber gloves, began to wash his hands. Sara covered the still form on the table with the sheet and then stood looking at Gray's broad shoulders and at his dark, bent head. A new passion of love for him swept over her. He stayed as sensitive as a boy, as capable of pity as the day he first took up his surgeon's scalpel, as merciless toward himself when he failed, even though success was hopeless, as it had been now. She longed to comfort him.

"After all, Lao Wang's chrysanthemums were what he loved best in the world," she said.

Gray answered her gruffly without turning around. "He ought to have had years more of living to love them, then."

They did not speak for a moment, each seeing the bent figure of the little old Chinese, squatting on his heels from spring when he began to pot chrysanthemum cuttings through summers of careful shading of the pots under awnings of matting and of careful watering and delicate manurings until autumn when, all weak buds carefully plucked off, his plants put forth their glorious flowers. Then proudly he would present to everyone whom he liked the flowers he thought appropriate. It was only yesterday morning that Sara had heard a cough at her door and, opening it, had found Lao Wang there, a pot in each arm and his brown wrinkled face smiling at her from between bouquets of enormous red and gold chrysanthemums. They would live in her window for many days, but he was dead.

Tears brimmed in her eyes and rolled quietly down her cheeks. Gray, turning suddenly, saw them.

"Sara!" He took two strides and flung his arm over her shoulder. "Dear Sara!"

"Life is so—so quickly gone," she whispered. "You love something terribly—like—like—chrysanthemums— and suddenly you can't love it any more because you're gone."

He was holding her harder than he knew. "It's this sort of death that is so beastly," he said passionately. "It's decent to die—properly—when you're old and things don't mean what they did, anyway. But to die because of something flung at you out of the sky—" He bit his lip, and she could feel him trembling against her. She wiped her eyes quickly.

"We're both tired," she said. She freed herself gently from his arm. If she had not she would have turned and put her head upon his breast, and that she must not. She had no right. All that could be hers was the comradeship of work with him. And how much that was! In the hours of day it was, she thought, enough. His work was his deepest life, and that she shared—and only she. Louise could never know what it meant to work with Gray, to stand beside him at the operating table, sharing in what his hands did with such speed and skill, sharing in the long talk of consultation and treatment. This was his real life and hers. But in the night when she put out her lonely lamp, it was more than she could do to look over to that southern corner of the compound and see the windows of Gray's house, still warmly bright. Where did a man live? Could any woman know?

Gray, watching her, thought, "Why did I do that? Why did I touch her? Something made me—it must not happen again."

He was troubled for a moment. Ought he to tell Louise? But there was nothing to tell her, simply that in a moment of impulse, because he had seen Sara's blue eyes dark under tears, he had put his arm about her shoulder. It was the sort of thing that men did to women anywhere, often, these days. He had seen it so in New York over and over again, always recoiling from it nevertheless, or himself stiffening under a woman's lingering touch upon him. He had lived so long here where men and women never touched each other except in private love.

"If there is no more to be done, I'll go home," he said, more brusquely than he knew. "Louise will be back from the shelter now. It's pretty hard on her, all this."

"It must be," Sara agreed listlessly.

He caught the tone of her voice. "Better go to bed early."

"I will—if nothing turns up," she agreed.

"If it does, send for me." But he regretted the words instantly. Louise did not like him to be sent for in the evening.

"Can't Sara take the evenings?" she had once inquired sharply. "What else has she to do?"

"I suppose she'd like a little rest," he had said.

"She looks as strong as a horse," Louise had said contemptuously.

"She isn't," he said, knowing while he did that Louise would go into silence for the rest of the evening if he took Sara's part. But the truth was instinct in him, and so he spoke it.

"I won't need to call you," Sara said.

They went out and he closed the door, and side by side they walked down the corridor of the hospital, quiet for the night. He thought of her lonely rooms and longed to say, "Come home with me—Louise will be glad to see you."

But he did not. Louise would not be glad to see her.

He knew that because he had tried it. He had taken Sara home with him and sat through an evening whose strangeness he could not to this day comprehend. Louise had been polite to Sara and more than usually demonstrative to him. She had looked very pretty that night. More than once he had caught Sara looking at Louise with bewildered eyes, half admiring, half hurt. But he himself was too bemused with Louise then. She was, that night, more like the girl he had fallen in love with in New York than he had seen her in months. And Sara had grown more and more silent, and at last she had got to her feet to say in her simple frank way:

"I must go home. I must leave you to yourselves. After all, you see so little of each other."

"Don't go, Sara," he had said, but there was the warmth of Louise's hand in his, of her blonde head leaning against his shoulder, of her amber eyes. And then, after Sara had gone, Louise had turned into her ordinary self instantly. She yawned, took her hand out of his to pat her lips and smooth her hair.

"Three's a stupid number," she had said. "You can't play bridge or do anything."

From the open window he had caught a glimpse of Sara walking solitary through the moonlight.

"Well, good night, Sara," he said now. They had reached the stairs.

"Good night, Gray."

"Got anything to read?"

She shook her head. "Nothing new. But I shan't read much."

He nodded without smiling because he yearned to do something for her and knew there was nothing he could do.

"Pity she can't meet some of those fellows down at the port," he thought. Down at the port there were half a dozen English and American men, and a couple of Europeans, Standard Oil, tobacco, businessmen, decent chaps, some of them, all womanless, except for what they might carry on with Chinese girls of low caste.

"Not that one of those fellows is good enough to look at Sara," he thought. He meditated sending her home on a furlough. But what would he do without her just now at the hospital? "I can't let her go just now," he decided, and opened the door of his own house.

. . . Sara at her own door paused. There was nothing in those three rooms, nothing but furniture, her few books and pictures. No one waited for her. Even Siu-mei, who sometimes slipped down the hall in the evening to come to her for talk, was at home tonight. She was restless with fatigue—no, with something deeper and incurable even by sleep. She knew what it was. She longed for Gray. Part of it was the simple longing of a woman for a man, but far beyond that there was the longing of one particular woman, herself, for him. She might, if she could, have gone to him straight and told him that she loved him. Had he been alone as she was alone she might have gone. But he was not alone. There was no possibility that he could love her. Why seek humiliation even of her love?

She sighed, opened the door and then left it ajar. Instead of going into the dark room, she went down the hall to the end of the corridor and opened another door. It was the door of the baby room. The babies were all quiet. Two had been born today. She turned up the low-burning night lamp and held it to see their little red-brown puckered faces—two perfectly healthy new human beings, born in the midst of the air raid. A bomb had burst just outside the hospital at the instant that the little boy cried, and she had not been able to hear his voice. But she could see that he was shouting at the world, his fists doubled and his dark-red body tense with his cries. Perhaps it was the same bomb that had ended Lao Wang's life.

She went on to the last cradle by the window. In it lay the motherless baby girl whom she had kept for her own, sleeping as quietly as the others. She had outgrown the puckishness of the newly born and was changing into a lovely little fragment of a woman.

"She is mine," Sara thought. She had said it aloud many times to others. She had said it to Gray. But for the first time she said it to herself. "The only baby I'll ever have," she thought. For if she could not have Gray's child she would bear no other.

She put down the lamp and turned it low again. Then she stooped and took up the little girl and went back to her room.

An hour later, while in Gray's house the lights still burned, she lay asleep upon her bed, in the curve of her arm, warm against her body, the little Chinese child.

. . . Gray thought, "I have never seen Louise so lovely."

He had dreaded coming home. He was late and, after the operation which had not saved Lao Wang, exhausted. And Louise after an air raid was sometimes hysterical and always ready for tears and comforting. He wanted comforting himself tonight.

But he saw immediately that something had happened to her. She was in the living room, reading, the couch drawn up to the small iron grate where a fire of Chinese coals burned with a fringe of blue flames. She had on a dress of soft yellow silk with long clinging sleeves and a low bosom, and her bright hair shone. Behind her the open doors into the dining room showed a table set with a white cloth and red chrysanthemums and red Chinese candles. She had not taken as much trouble as that for a long time. Left to himself, Siao Fah never put flowers on the table. Why, he reasoned, when they were not to be eaten? And why candles, when there was the lamp? Siao Fah, watching Louise arrange the table, had perfectly understood all she did, as well as the yellow dress. "She is guilty," he thought with pleasure.

She looked anything but guilty as Gray bent over her to kiss her. A warm sweet perfume was in her hair.

"Darling, you grow prettier in spite of all the hardship," he said. "I never saw you prettier even at a New York dinner party. Sure you don't mind there's only me to see you?"

"If I minded, I wouldn't be here," she said, smiling. She loved him and knew it. She would not have stayed a day had she not loved him. But she wanted to live with him in her own world, where there was ease and security and gaiety and people to admire her and her successful marriage to Gray Thomison, the only son of the Thomisons of New York and half a dozen other places. She could see the sort of home she wanted in New York, the house that she and Gray were used to and could afford. To live in this little Chinese house in the corner of a hospital compound would have been absurd in the best of times. Under the daily rain of bombs it was madness. Her task was to persuade him that he must leave this miserable country. He could be a great doctor in New York, she thought, a doctor, young, handsome, able. He was handsome, she thought, her blood prickling a little as she looked up at him. He was easily the handsomest man she had ever seen.

"Lift me up," she said, holding up her arms.

He lifted her up and she clung limp against him. The kitchen door opened, and Siao Fah put in his head, saw, snarled soundlessly, and shut the door again.

"Oh, my wife!" Gray whispered. All over his body nerves, taut and braced, relaxed and let down. If Louise could always be like this! He smoothed her hair with trembling tenderness. "Was the raid too bad today, sweet? I was operating and didn't know." He decided not to tell her that Lao Wang had died.

"It was pretty bad, but maybe I am getting used to it. Dr. Chung was nice about helping me."

"That's good, sweet. I'm glad, so long as I can't be there."

He wished that he had not said that, because she never understood why he felt he must stay with the sure-to-dies. He and Sara always stayed. But she did not protest. She clung to him a moment. Then she kissed him.

"Change for dinner, will you, Gray?"

"Sure I will—what's this, an anniversary?"

She shook her head brightly. "No, I just feel like it."

"All the more reason." He pulled her along with him. "The moment this wretched bombing is over, sweet, we must have a little fun—get some of the men up from the port for dinner. Maybe one of them will fall for Sara, eh? Not a bad idea?"

"Not at all," she agreed. She had met the men from the port. They had come to call one rainy day when it seemed sure no planes could fly. But they had not stayed for dinner. They were responsible for their concerns.

"There's always some fool who delays to pick up one more precious belonging," one of the men had said. She had liked him the best of all—Harry Delafield. "I nearly lost our best compradore last week because of his canary. He'd forgotten it and toddled back under fire to fetch it out of his office."

No, dinners were not possible in air raids. She thought exultingly, "But if there really aren't any more air raids?"

For that afternoon, after two hours of it, she had turned to Dr. Chung. He had stood beside her the whole time. Once she had seized his arm when a bomb burst just outside the shelter. The concussion sucked the air out of her lungs, and her head whirled.

"I can't bear this," she had thought, "I simply can't bear it."

The Chinese seemed to understand. In the first silence he had turned to her, though at the sight of his dark, opaque eyes her hand dropped from his arm. He did not notice. He said in his kindest voice:

"You cannot bear this."

"No," she agreed. Her lashes fluttered. "So, Dr. Chung, you know—what we were talking about—I will do it."

He bowed gravely and with dignity. And half an hour ago he had brought her a letter written on plain white paper. She read it quickly. It was nothing, a simple informal note.

DEAR HARRY:

We are all well and happy. I hope you reached home safely. Your visit did us good. Sorry that you will not be coming again soon.

As ever,

She took up her pen and signed her name, Louise Thomison.

Dr. Chung took the paper from her hands. "This means safety for you and for the hospital," he had said gently, and bowed himself away.

Of course she would tell Gray sometime, she thought, some day when it was all over. Maybe she could even tell him that it was she who had saved the hospital—saved them all. She felt gay for the first time since she had come to Chen-li.

. . . As for Dr. Chung, he was at this moment watching for the hospital gate to open. It was a new gate, and the pillars were repaired and the sign put up again, "The House of Mercy." Siu-mei was late, but he was too triumphant to be tired. He had the letter in his pocket, and he would as soon as he had seen Siu-mei take it to Yasuda for proof that he had done what he said he would.

A little before midnight the gate opened, and Siu-mei's riksha came in. In the light of the lanterns by the gate he saw her step down and pay the man, and then come into the hospital. He went down the steps, timing himself so that she might see him gracefully descending them. She saw him and stood at their foot, waiting for him. There was no one near to be seen, but he chose to speak in English, lest there be a waiting ear. Siu-mei knew English and spoke it with a pretty, faltering accent.

"Did you talk with your father?"

"Yes," she said, smiling at him.

"So he knows?"

"Yes," she said.

"And approves?"

She was about to say, "Of course," and then hesitated. "Strangely, the air raid began just as he was about to answer me," she said.

"And you did not speak of it afterward?"

"I forgot he had not—approved," she said, ashamed. And then when she saw his face she said, "But *I* approve —and that is enough for him."

He took her hand at that and she let it lie on his. He lifted it, palm upward, and smelled it delicately in caress.

"Your hand is like a lotus bud," he said.

They had stood for a quivering moment, when they heard a cough. There stood Ya-ching, the pock-marked nurse. Her face was blank.

"The Japanese says he cannot sleep," she said.

"I will come," Chung said coldly.

And, though Siu-mei would have pulled her hand away, he held it, and now he pressed it as if in Western parting.

"Good night," he said distinctly.

"Good night," Siu-mei replied.

Behind him the nurse Ya-ching turned and gave her

a look so full of hate that she stood still for a long moment, as though she had been stabbed, and later in her bed lay sleepless, the look still sharp in her as a knife.

. . . She could not forget the look until a few days later . . . when in the maternity ward she looked up startled at a tall young man in a faded blue uniform. Then her pretty face turned severe and in the instant she forgot herself. He was Chen-ta Eagle, and she recognized him and felt no less severe.

"What are you doing here, you man?" she demanded. "This is a place for women only."

"By my mother, I have no wish to be here," he replied. "But where am I? I came in the door and walked and walked and here I am."

"You should have announced yourself to someone, or asked for Thomison doctor or Chung doctor."

They missed Lao Wang, who, pottering in the garden had seen all who came and went. She had thought of him only a few minutes ago as she looked out of a window in passing. A frost had killed the chrysanthemums during the night. It had been always the saddest day of the year when that happened. Lao Wang gave up the garden until spring. But this year he did not know its coming, nor would he know the return of spring.

"Why should I announce myself to anyone I chanced to see?" Chen-ta asked.

His bold black eyes rested with pleasure on Siu-mei. She was the prettiest girl he had ever seen, and he had remembered her from the night the white woman had sewed up the ripped belly of his prisoner.

"What is your name?" he asked.

She pretended not to hear him. "What do you want?" she demanded.

"Your name."

The women in the ward laughed. Everybody was cheerful. This was the third day that there had been no planes above the hospital. There were raids, but the planes soared high over these buildings and dropped their bombs on the far side of the city.

"*O-mi-to-fu,*" old Chinese men and women murmured. "Buddha wakes at last."

Sick people slept more easily and ate their food with gratitude for peace of any kind, even though it must end.

"My name is my own," Siu-mei said, her face grave at the Eagle's impudence. "I give it to no man."

"You will force me to take it, then," he replied with unmoved good humor. "It is my rule to take what I want if it is not given me."

"Be silent," she commanded him, "and follow me." She led him away from the laughing women into the corridor. "Stop your joking and tell me why you are here."

"Why? To take back my Japanese captive, of course," he cried. "Is he cured?"

"How should I know?" she replied. "I have nothing to do with the men."

"Here is one with whom you may have anything to do that you will," he said instantly.

She tried not to laugh and failed. "Will you cease jesting?" she cried, covering her smiling mouth with her hand. "Come with me to Thomison doctor. He decides everything here."

She turned without giving him a chance for more impudence, and he followed, admiring her slender shape and swift sure tread.

"You could climb the hills as well as any man," he exclaimed.

She did not answer this. She marched along, her head high and laughter in her heart.

"Here is Thomison doctor's office," she said. "I will tell him. Wait here."

She went in to find Gray at his desk, sitting unusually idle, a frown upon his face. He stared at someone behind her. She turned and found the Eagle behind her. She stamped her foot.

"I told you to wait!" she cried.

"Why should I wait?" he replied calmly. "I do not obey women."

He sat down coolly and loosened the girdle of blue cloth about his waist and opened his shirt over his smooth brown breast.

"It is too hot in your hospital," he told Gray pleasantly.

"The patients require some warmth," Gray replied.

"This man's Chen-ta, the Eagle," Siu-mei said. "He comes for the Japanese."

"Is that son of evil well again?" Chen-ta asked. "I have come thirty miles to fetch him."

"He is well," Gray replied. "But he has been the patient of my colleague, and I must consult him."

"Shall I tell Dr. Chung?" Siu-mei asked quickly.

"If you will," Gray replied.

Chen-ta held his peace until she had gone. Then he cleared his throat.

"Does she have a husband?" he asked.

Gray did not answer for a second, not knowing indeed how to answer.

"I do not know her affairs," he replied at last as coldly as he could, for he wanted to laugh. The man was a brave-looking fellow, handsome as heroes ought to look and seldom did. He was famous over these provinces for his daring attacks upon the enemy, darting at them under cover of darkness, out of hidden valleys, from seemingly innocent villages. But he looked ruthless. Gray made his face serious.

"One promise I must exact if this man is given back to you," he said.

"What is it?" Chen-ta asked.

"That you do not kill him."

"Are Americans friends of the Japanese, that they always ask this?" Chen-ta demanded. His broad black brows flew upward. "The white woman asked me this also when I brought him here."

"No, we are not," Gray said. "How could we be when we see what they have done? Look for yourself at the ruin in our compound and see if we can be friends with them. But we do not like our patients to be killed."

"To me it seems very peaceful in this place," Chen-ta said, looking about the quiet room.

"For the last three days we have had peace."

"Why?"

"What can it be but accident? They were here yesterday, but they flew high over us. Stay a few hours longer, and you will see."

"I cannot. My men are waiting at the Pine Tree Pass. As for my promise, I give it. I will not kill the Japanese. He is no common fellow. I have use for him."

"What use?"

"Why should I tell you?"

"Because his life belongs to us. He would have died had we not healed him."

"Healing is your business. Has he not paid you?"

"He has paid us money, but how can money pay for life?"

Chen-ta sat frowning at the white man. "I will tell you this much: he shall be fed and sheltered and his life will be safe."

"Torture?"

"No torture," Chen-ta declared. "My prisoners are not

tortured. What am I in your eyes? I kill quickly or I save alive. This one I save alive."

"For what purpose?" Gray asked again.

"For my purpose," Chen-ta replied again.

"I ask one more thing," Gray said. "Is it a good purpose?"

The two men looked at each other for a steady moment. Then Chen-ta put his big hands on his knees and leaned forward, his eyes fast upon Gray's.

"Do you know the purpose of your life in this place?"

"Assuredly I do," Gray replied.

"Then you know mine, also," Chen-ta said.

"I like this fellow," Gray was thinking. "This is a good man. No one but a good man would have a face like his."

"You may take your prisoner if Dr. Chung allows it," he said aloud. "I trust all you have said." He glanced at the door. It was strange, he thought, that Siu-mei had not returned. He rose. "Wait here, and I will go and see whether he is to be brought to you."

When he opened the door of Yasuda's room, Siu-mei was standing beside the bed. On the other side stood Dr. Chung, his watch in his hand, his thumb and finger upon Yasuda's wrist.

"See for yourself," he told Siu-mei. "I cannot give a reason for this relapse."

A little to one side behind him stood the nurse Ya-ching. Under her immobile square face her mind was moiling with hatred of Siu-mei. She had been jealous of

Siu-mei from the day Siu-mei entered the hospital, not to become a nurse, but a doctor, since she was the daughter of a rich man. From Siu-mei she had had each year to take more and more often orders and requests. It made no difference that Siu-mei's voice was courteous and soft, and that she was considerate, or that she ignored Ya-ching's moodiness. Ya-ching hated her for these very reasons, as she hated her smooth peach-colored cheeks and her great black eyes. Long before Chung had known that he loved Siu-mei, Ya-ching knew it would come about because it was the thing she feared above all else. What one feared always came true, she thought savagely. She went to the temple and burned incense to the gods of Death and prayed for Siu-mei's death. But Siu-mei did not die. One after another Ya-ching gave gifts to the gods of smallpox and leprosy and decay of the lungs and liver and of broken bones and fevers, but Siu-mei continued to bloom. And then, in her despairing passion for the handsome young doctor, Ya-ching began to let him know her secret. In all the small ways that a desperate, hungry woman approaches a man, Ya-ching approached Chung and laid bare her heart before him, careless of anything except his favor. Her face was pock-marked and her skin pallid and thick, and her features were coarse and her eyebrows sparse. But, despite this ugly face, her body was beautiful, a shapely thing, the skin smooth and untouched by scars. Yet what was this body to her if it must remain forever unseen?

And then she knew herself repulsed. The man she loved so that her love ate up her heart and her thoughts ignored that which he could not fail to see. He did not see her hand when it must touch his, her eyes speaking what her lips yearned to tell, nor care that the body nearer his than need be was beautiful. She rolled her sleeves high in pretended zeal when she worked for him, that he might see her smooth white arms. If he saw them he gave no sign.

She had had a last faint joy when he bade her take care of the Japanese who was his patient. But the joy had soon passed. For it only gave her the chance to see him more often, and in him the shaping of love, never for her, but for Siu-mei. Thus she stood, watching these two, seemingly aware only of what they did; but she saw their eyes and the warm color of Siu-mei's cheeks.

"The pulse is certainly too swift," Siu-mei said. "And the heart beat is strangely faint. Was he as usual last night?"

"He seemed almost entirely well," Chung said.

Yasuda lay, looking from one to the other, panting. He felt very ill indeed and a little frightened. Now that he had swallowed the pills, he was confused as to whether he had not taken too many. Four, Chung had said, if he put his hand to his mouth when he came in the door. That signified haste. Surely he had said four? Or was it only three? He felt weak and breathless, and the two faces near him dimmed in his eyes.

"Water," he whispered.

"Water," Chung repeated to Ya-ching.

She poured a bowlful from a clay jug on the table. But when Chung lifted the sick man's head he could not drink. He had fainted.

"What is this?" Siu-mei cried.

"Who can tell?" Chung replied, laying Yasuda down. He handed the still brimming cup back to Ya-ching.

And at that moment Gray came to the door. "I have been looking for you, Chung," he began. Then he caught sight of Yasuda. "What's wrong?"

"We don't know," Chung replied.

"But the man's dying!" Gray cried. "Quick, a hypodermic!"

Chung turned to Ya-ching, and she left the room. Gray looked impatiently at her slow heavy tread. "You go, Siu-mei—minutes count."

Siu-mei went, passing Ya-ching in the hall. "Never mind," she called. "I have one here in my office."

Ya-ching paused and stood still, her face a mask of hate, and then went back to the room.

There Gray was throwing questions at Chung, and Chung shrugged his shoulders.

"It is as you see it," he said. "I know nothing. Some internal complication."

"Did he know that his captor had come?" Gray asked.

Chung shook his head. "Who had told him? I have not spoken a word to him."

"Strange," Gray was muttering, "strange—strange!"

Siu-mei came back in an instant with the hypodermic, and Gray plunged it into Yasuda's arm. They stood and watched the ashen face. It remained perfectly still. Then at last the lips quivered, the eyelids moved, and Yasuda's opaque gray-black eyes saw returning shapes of faces about him.

"Water," he whispered hoarsely. "Water."

"Give him all he can drink," Gray commanded abruptly. He waited while Ya-ching held the bowl to his lips. Then he tested Yasuda's pulse and heart and examined his eyelids. "This man is certainly too sick to be moved now," he declared. "Chung, I would not leave him yet if I were you."

"I will not," Chung agreed.

"Call me if you need me," Gray continued.

"I think there will be no need," Chung replied.

When Gray had gone away, he turned to Siu-mei. "Do not wait," he said. "I will come to your office and tell you how he is."

She gave him a warm quick look as she went, and Ya-ching caught it as it passed. She stood until Siu-mei had gone. She waited in silence while Chung walked to the window and lit a cigarette.

"Arrange the patient's bed," he ordered her, and stood with his back to her scanning the sky. It was a bright blue day, the air still and the heavens cloudless. Even as he stood, the warning siren shrieked across the silence.

An air raid, he thought, but without terror. This was the third day of peace in the hospital.

"The patient must not be moved," he said calmly.

"So," Ya-ching replied. At that moment her hand came upon something under Yasuda's pillow. She drew it out and looked at it. It was a small ball of hastily crumpled paper. She held it in her shut hand. Then the siren shrieked again. She glared at Chung's turned back, at Yasuda's closed eyes, and opened the paper. In it were some small sulphur-colored pills. She was about to cry out, and then she did not. Over her face crept a secret and triumphant look. She thrust the pills into her bosom and went on making the bed.

In the office Chen-ta stared at Gray. "Here is a strange thing," he said. "First a man is well and then he is ill."

"It is as strange to me as to you," Gray replied. "But it is so."

"When am I to return for him, then?"

"Give him three days more," Gray said.

The siren sounded for air raid. Chen-ta rose. "Three days, then," he shouted.

"Three days," Gray shouted back. "And you had better stay until this is over!"

Chen-ta shook his head. "If I had feared those eggs they drop, I would have been dust long ago!" he bawled. Then he turned and strode from the room and down the hall and out of the hospital. He was too busy to heed the approaching planes. He was full of wonder at himself and at his good temper. Why was he not angry at this delay, he who was always quickly angry at anything that happened against his will? Why was he even pleased at the thought of returning here in three days? He searched himself and knew the reason. In his memory he saw that pretty face of the tall girl who had led him to the white doctor's office. Siu-mei, the white man had called her, too familiarly, he thought with indignation. Then he was further astonished. Why should he care if one called her Siu-mei? In his bemusement he saw without notice a man in blue coat and trousers approach and dart aside into a door before he came near. If he had been himself Chen-ta would have leaped after him to look at him and see who wished to escape him. But now, though he thought vaguely that he knew the fellow, he let him go. He went his own way back to his hills, every now and again in the midst of exploding bombs stopping to look dazed and to scratch his head.

"What is this that has befallen me!" he cried. His big voice was soundless in the roaring about him. But it was his own voice he heard nevertheless, and not the noise of the falling bombs.

. . . Chung Third, darting among the shadows of the walls, hid in a clump of bamboos until Chen-ta's sturdy shape had gone through the hospital gate. Then he went quietly up the back stairs of the hospital and through winding back corridors until he reached his brother's room. He did not knock or cough, but opened the door without a sound. Chung was there, standing at his table, his back to the door. Chung Third whispered, "Elder Brother!"

Chung leaped and turned. In his hand he held a mortar and pestle. "Why do you enter like a thief?" he cried angrily.

Chung Third opened his eyes wide. "How do I know when you are doing what you do not wish known?" he answered smartly.

"Be silent, you rabbit!" Chung swore at him.

Chung Third looked stubborn. "Shall I tell you what I know or shall I keep it to myself?" He hated this elder brother of his, but still they were one blood. He would not betray him easily, yet why should he pretend that he was ignorant of his doings?

"Well, what?" Chung said impatiently. On the table was a piece of soft Chinese paper, and upon the paper a few small yellow pills. Chung Third stared at them.

"What are those?" he asked.

"Is it your business?" Chung retorted. "Say what you have to say."

Chung Third shrugged himself. "Well, then, the next attack is tomorrow night, thirty-two miles east from here and seventeen miles north. This is the path of the Eagle." He put on the table a piece of red paper such as sweet cakes are wrapped in, and upon it were brushed roads and the names of villages.

Chung did not look at it. He was now crushing together again the powders in the mortar he held. "Leave it here," he said.

"Is there nothing else?" Chung Third asked.

"Nothing," Chung replied.

"For me there is something," Chung Third said doggedly. He spat on the polished wooden floor, and Chung threw him a furious look. But he said nothing. He opened a drawer and took out some money and put it on the map.

"There is your price," he said with scorn.

But Chung Third only laughed as he put the money in his bosom. He pulled his hat somewhat more over his left ear and went away more cheerful than he entered. Outside in the corridor he saw a woman standing as though she waited. For whom, he wondered? And then he saw her face. For no one, with such a face as hers, he decided, and forgot her, in his own content. He had what he had earned, and he was not always so lucky.

V

IN HIS KITCHEN Siao Fah ordered his nephew about in a surly tone. It had been necessary to have help in the house since his mistress had changed herself into this woman she now was. He understood the change sometimes, and sometimes he did not. Every few days, perhaps even one day following another, Chung doctor came to the house, always when Thomison doctor was away. At such times Siao Fah put aside anything he was doing, even to the ruin of one of his best soufflés, and placed his three-legged stool at the keyhole. But inside the living room the same thing always happened—that is, nothing. The Chinese man gave the white woman a sheet of paper, and she wrote something from it upon another piece. That was all. Then the man bowed and the woman smiled. Sometimes they spoke a few words. Once he was greatly excited because the man brought with him a green pottery bowl of sacred lilies in full bloom. But they meant nothing, it seemed, for she put them on the table, and then they stayed there until they faded and he himself threw them away.

"Wash rice!" he shouted at his nephew, Little Pig.

Little Pig, who was an undersized boy of fourteen with an elderly face, obeyed instantly. He was given to chatter, but he knew when silence was safer. It was when his uncle looked like this. There were times when Siao Fah's temper would have made Little Pig run away from this job to which his parents had apprenticed him, except that he was able to steal so much food here. White sugar he had never tasted in his life until he came to this house. Now, whenever he went to the cupboard in the passageway, and he made many excuses to go there, he wet his forefinger in his mouth and dipped it deep into the sugar and licked it off clean. He was able to do this seven or eight times before he felt his uncle might notice his absence. Then he would return, looking industrious with a dish towel over his shoulder. There was only one good thing about this mistress, Siao Fah said often, and it was that she never came into the kitchen.

"At least she knows how ignorant she is," Siao Fah said loudly to Little Pig. "She leaves the affairs of my master's stomach to me. It is I who keep him strong and alive." The last time he said this he had squinted at the sky and added, "Now that the Japs avoid striking us."

It was a thing no one pretended to understand, this peace over the hospital; and now, after twelve days, everyone felt it more than strange.

"Who could have thought peace could be sinister?" Gray was saying at that moment to Sara.

They stood together at the wide window of the laboratory on the second floor, looking across to the hills. It was clear dusk on a late winter's afternoon, this mild winter of Chen-li, which seldom deepened to ice or snow. Across the purple-black of the mountains the wavering firefly lights were climbing upward. But the people of Chen-li still had no peace.

"It is beginning to be rumored in the city that only the hospital compound is always safe," Sara said. "Have you noticed, the last few days, how people come into the compound after the first warning?"

"Yes," Gray said shortly. He had seen, and he had not liked it. Tonight, as he was dressing for one of Louise's little dinner parties, the siren had screamed, and he threw his topcoat on over shirt and trousers to come at once to the hospital. There was always the chance that the planes might hover over the hospital again. And on the way he had seen figures, indistinct in the darkness, moving to avoid his notice. He caught a group of them with his flashlight and saw a little family, man, woman, and two children. They stood immobile, statues in the light. The man must have been from a smithy, for his face and hands were black with iron and coal dust.

"Whom are you seeking?" Gray had asked gently. A sort of tenderness made him always mild now with these people. They suffered daily with such silent patience that who could be angry with them, whatever they did?

"We seek no one," the man said in apology, "only a little safety, Thomison doctor."

"Stay, then, if you find it here," he had replied. He went on, stopping to look at no one else, and had come straight to find Sara. She was in the laboratory examining slides.

"Why in hell aren't we being bombed?" he had asked her.

"I ask you the same question," she replied. "Shall we take our people to shelter or not?" Day after day this had to be decided.

"They made such a damned row about it yesterday," he said reluctantly. "Nobody wanted to go. They all talked about Buddha having come to protect them at last. There's a lot of rot about the air above us being crystallized so that the bombs glance off. They are always ready to believe in miracles."

"Let's risk it tonight?" Sara suggested.

The second warning sounded.

"It would be hell if the Japs changed their minds," he said soberly.

"It's a ghastly responsibility," she admitted.

Thus they stood, side by side at the window, staring at the mountains. The minutes sped, one after another, and they did not speak or move, sharing the responsibility between them. The last warning sounded.

"It is too late now," Gray said.

"Yes," she agreed.

Far above them they could see the lights of the approaching planes. In ten minutes, in five, they would know whether they were right or wrong.

"I hope we are blown to bits with the rest if we're wrong," Gray said grimly.

"Yes," Sara said again.

She moved nearer to him, and he put out his hand and found hers and held it hard. Neither put into words the communion that flowed between them. For him it was not like any he had with Louise. Therefore it was not love. And yet he knew, to his alarm, that his feeling for Sara was not what it had been. She had become a woman to him. He saw against his will the shape of her tender mouth and the droop of her lids at the corners of her dark-blue eyes. How could he see these things when he loved Louise? He put the question away in self-disgust without answering it. But for Sara this communion was everything, and she took it with proud gratitude. Then Gray spoke. "I'm glad I don't have to go through this alone."

She did not answer. The sound of her own voice would break the moment. She wanted only to take from him all that he could give her.

"They are passing," Gray said. He dropped her hand lightly without pressure and threw open the window and leaned out. "Passing us clean, by George!"

He stared at the sky for a long moment and then he shut the window and turned to her, bewildered. "God, I don't know whether to be glad or sorry," he said slowly.

"Nor I," she said, and put all her sad heart into the secrecy of words. To die with Gray, to live without him —it was a choice she was glad that she did not have to make.

He went away without saying more, frowning as he went and tramping down the hall toward the hospital door. The siren was sounding for safety, and Louise would be expecting him. Her guests might even be there. She had invited four men from the port, and usually they came early to avoid the hour of nightly raids.

He walked quickly across the winter-bitten grass, paying no heed to the quiet people who were now leaving the hospital compound. Let them share this inexplicable safety, if it had to be. He was beginning to feel it somehow shameful.

"I've got to get at the bottom of this," he thought angrily, marching up his own steps. It would have to be tomorrow, though, he knew, as he opened the door. A burst of men's voices fell upon his ears, and above them like high music he heard Louise's laughter.

. . . In the low-ceiled living room of the Chinese house Louise was beginning to be able to forget for such hours as these all that she did not want to remember— the hospital, the city lying close between river and mountains, the narrow crowded streets, the people among whom she was so alien, whose very looks she hated. Yesterday Gray had made her take a walk with him and had stopped for a moment to watch a baby boy just able to walk. The cobbles were wet, the baby slipped and put out his hand to catch at her skirt to save himself a fall. She had drawn back, her instinct quick, and the child had fallen.

"Louise!" Gray had cried, and then he stooped to pick up the sobbing child.

She had stood without a word while he dusted off the child's padded red garments and while he led him to a candy vendor's stall and bought him a stick of barley toffee coated with sesame seeds. By then the child's mother had come running out of a small hot water shop. She knew Gray, as everybody seemed to, and she was full of smiles and chatter. Gray had said nothing afterward for a while, and then he had asked her outright:

"Louise, why did you draw back from a child?"

"Because it was Chinese, I suppose," she said clearly. "I don't need to defend myself," she thought.

"Why do you hate them?" he asked.

"They disgust me," she said coldly. "I can't help it. I can't bear to have them touch me, even the children."

"And I love them," he said slowly. "I admire them and find them brave and full of humor and courage and all that I like people to be."

She did not answer this, nor did he say more. But they walked along the Chinese streets very far from each other. And when she got home she had written an impulsive little note to Harry Delafield at the port.

I'm a little low, dear Harry. Bring your men along and have dinner with us tomorrow. We're very safe to dine with these days, you know—thanks to the whimsical enemy.

LOUISE

She was not quite sure that Gray knew that she and Harry called each other by their first names. There was no reason why they should not, except Harry's English formality.

"Gray won't mind," she had urged him last week. "Go on, Harry."

"Hang it, I can't," Harry had said frankly. "It's odd that when we're alone, you and I, I can say 'Louise' as easily as anything. But the minute he's there it sticks in my throat. I can only gasp out 'Mrs. Thomison.' I say!"

"What?" she asked, laughing at him.

"You don't think I'm falling in love with you, do you?"

"I can't tell you," she replied, laughing more than ever at his grave face.

"I say, it would be very awkward if I were—the Service doesn't at all like that sort of thing. Stop me if you notice anything, will you? There's a good girl!"

She enjoyed him enormously, this smart-looking young Englishman who was obviously in training to be promoted to a higher post, and had been sent to the "interior" for experience. But she enjoyed altogether the piquancy of being the only white woman, and a very

124

pretty one, among famished white men. It was her one pleasure in Chen-li. She was perfectly safe, she was married, and she could let them fall a little in love with her, each in his own way, and herself only be better satisfied with Gray, handsomer, more keen, more intelligent than any of them. She was always warmer to him after such evenings as this.

And Gray, coming in, greeted them and excused himself to go away and finish dressing. In his room alone he savored the scene he had just left. The room was lighted by Chinese candles and the coal fire full of warmth and invitation. Louise, in a bright green velvet frock, a wide gold girdle about her waist, had never looked more beautiful. Her eyes, when she was happy, glowed with amber light, and her fine fair hair sprang electrically from her face. No wonder the four men hovered over her! He smiled, not in the least jealous. If Louise could find a little fun, bless her, let her find it, he thought. It was only a pity that she would never have Sara here. He always felt uncomfortable about that, but he had given up trying to change Louise. A shame, when Sara was so young and good-looking and had so little fun! He made up his mind to speak about it again.

It was at this moment that he noticed the handle of his door turning silently and slowly. He waited, a pearl stud in his hand. The door opened, and Siao Fah put in his head. When he saw Gray was alone, he came in and shut the door and stood against it.

"I have something to say to you," he whispered.

"Say it, then," Gray replied. "Why need you be so secret?"

"It's about her." He jerked his chin in the direction of Louise's bed.

"Well?" Gray's voice was cold. He knew very well that Siao Fah did not like Louise. It was, he supposed, because Louise complained of dust under things. Siao Fah was a good cook, but no hand at cleaning. Since Louise would learn no Chinese and Siao Fah stubbornly pretended to understand not a word of English, Gray was their means of communication. Their last argument had resulted in the hiring of Little Pig, who was told only to clean.

"She is not worthy of you." Siao Fah pursed his mouth and clasped his hands behind his back.

"Perhaps I can judge that better than you," Gray replied. "Go on back to your kitchen. Why do you talk about such things now, while the dinner burns, doubtless?"

"I have arranged the dinner," Siao Fah replied. "I come now because I have waited for days to speak to you alone. You are with her always."

"Naturally, since she is my wife," Gray replied.

"What would you say if I gave you a letter written to another man?"

"I would not believe it," Gray said impatiently. "Get out of my sight, you cook-boy!" He was fond of Siao

Fah, but this was too much, he thought indignantly. He would be compelled to let him go.

And then he saw Siao Fah's hand go into his bosom and bring out an envelope, and he saw Siao Fah take out a letter. It was Louise's writing. He knew that big loose handwriting which looked so clear and was so hard to read. He made up his mind that he would not take the letter, and then took it. He determined not to open it, not to read it, and then he did open it and did read it, at a glance. It was very short, a few lines and her name.

DEAREST HARRY:

I have not been very well, and fear I shall not be for a long time in this atmosphere. I long to leave and yet must stay. Come to me day after tomorrow. No one will be here then. The safest hour is midafternoon. As long as you can come to me, I can bear my life.

LOUISE

He read it again and again, as though he could not stop reading it.

"Where did you get it?" he whispered.

"She writes these letters," Siao Fah said, "and the Chinese doctor brings her others."

"Chung?" Gray cried, not believing.

Siao Fah nodded. "That one."

"But what letters does he bring her?"

"That I do not know," Siao Fah said with dignity. "I do not understand English."

"Still you do not tell me how you got this letter," Gray demanded.

"When she answers the letters which Chung brings her, I carry the answer in my basket with the letters you give her to post when I go every day to market. She puts your chop on the letters. See?" He turned the envelope over to show Gray, and there was his Chinese seal.

"But—but," Gray stammered, "there is no meaning to this! Chung brings her letters, she writes others—"

"Master, it is like this: From someone Chung brings her letters, always when you are not here. Then she writes and puts it in my basket with your letters that I take to the post office when I go to market. Do you ever look in my basket? Why should you do so? It is expected that your wife is honorable."

"Go back to your kitchen," Gray said.

"Yes, master," Siao Fah replied, and most docilely. Now he had done his duty, he thought. He went back to the kitchen and found Little Pig with his fingers in the gravy and clapped him on the head with the iron spoon he took to stir the soup before he served it.

"Pig and son of a pig!" he said, severe with his own righteousness.

In his room Gray put the letter in his drawer and went on dressing carefully. In the mirror his face was very white, and his dark eyes stared back at him.

"Steady," he was saying to himself, "no jumping at conclusions." And yet who was "dearest Harry" except the Harry there in his own living room? "I ought to be able to see for myself tonight," he thought thickly. Queer how he could scarcely think at all! His head was pounding as though an engine had been set going in it. He sat down a moment when he was dressed, wondering if he were going to be sick.

Louise came to the door. "What's wrong, Gray?"

"I have a beastly headache."

"Oh, Gray, I am sorry! Want anything?"

"Bring me a nip of whisky, will you?"

"Of course."

She came back in a moment, her long green gown trailing behind her, the small glass held daintily in her white fingers.

"Here you are, poor boy." She touched his forehead with those fingers, and he shivered and drank. Then he rose to his feet.

"Better?" she asked.

"Yes."

"Sure you want to come out?"

"Of course," he said shortly.

. . . She shrugged her shoulders at Harry a moment later and drew down her pretty scarlet mouth. "Poor Gray has such a headache," she said in her softest voice.

"I say, how rotten, old chap!" Harry cried.

"Too bad"—"too bad," the other men echoed.

"Do you have them often, Thomison?" Harry persisted. He liked Louise's husband very much, and sometimes thought her not good enough for him. He did not like her the less himself for that, preferring women who were not too good. "I hope it'll be better," he said earnestly without waiting for Gray's answer.

"It won't be," Gray said, permitting himself a touch of bitterness. "It's one of those things which must be worse before it can be better," he said.

. . . He watched, without seeming to, the evening through, the play between Louise and Harry. The other men were nothing but a silent, attentive background for the sparkling, the laughter, the banter between these two. Jones, the *taipan* of the oil company, corpulent and kind; Lennard, his second in command; and Blackman, of a Virginia tobacco firm, took their parts, enjoying without envy their pretty hostess. Siao Fah had done his best, after all, and the dinner was very good. He had found pheasants that were less mangled with shot than Chinese hunters usually left them and had roasted them slowly over coals and had stuffed them with chestnuts. The food was a harmony of all the materials and flavors that Siao Fah had collected from the markets of Chen-li, into which fish from the river and game from the hills and fowl and vegetables from village farms were daily poured, in spite of war. But there was no butter and no coffee. Foods from abroad had ceased. And the little feathery rolls had the faintly sharp flavor of Chinese yeast.

"This might be anywhere," Harry said, grateful with well-being after dinner. He had brought a box of Havana cigars, a gift from an English gunboat captain, and now he gave them to Siao Fah to pass to the men.

"Thanks, I'll smoke my pipe," Gray said. He wanted blindly to talk to Sara, to ask her what to do if Louise meant what she looked and smiled and said in every response she made to this other man.

. . . "Did you say anything to Louise?" Sara asked.

She had known the moment Gray came into the hospital this morning that something was wrong. Her instinct toward him was delicate and quick. He had come into her office frowning, and for a moment she had thought it only anxiety over Yasuda. None of them could diagnose Yasuda's illness.

"I'm about ready to make an exploratory operation on him," Gray said without greeting. He sat down. "I'd do it today if I weren't all in," he went on. Then he smiled wryly. "But it wouldn't be fair to cut up even a Jap when I'm feeling like this."

"What's wrong?" she inquired. "Peace?"

"That's bad enough," he said. "What's that story about the fellow who cried peace, peace, when there was no peace? Well, this is worse—peace when there oughtn't to be peace. No, it's not that . . . Sara!"

"Yes, Gray?" She had put down the new budget upon which she had been working and leaned her chin on her hands and looked at him. Her eyes, he saw suddenly, were very wide apart—too wide, perhaps? Or was it simply that he was used to Louise's eyes? He looked away from Sara.

"It's about Louise."

She did not answer this.

He went on, "She's—been lonely, of course. She doesn't get the excitement you and I have in this work we do—doesn't get any fun out of it. Not everybody can."

"Of course not," she said.

"So maybe it's nothing but harmless playing about. People did that sort of thing a lot at home, I noticed. I've lived too long here, maybe, where everything between a man and a woman is—serious."

She did not answer again, waiting.

Gray twisted in his chair. "So, well—this is what Siao Fah gave me last night."

Then he took the letter from his pocket and handed it to her, and while she read it he thought of Louise. Louise had been more than usually affectionate last night. When they were alone again she had curled into his lap, still laughing.

"Wasn't it fun, Gray?" she said.

"Great fun."

"Harry's such a goose."

"A goose very fond of you, I think!"

She heard the jealousy in his voice and treasured it triumphantly. Jealousy could be a weapon in the right hand!

"Well, a goose, anyway!" she had said. Then she had leaned her head on his shoulder and shut her eyes. "Oh, but I'm tired!"

And he had sat holding her, her fair hair spread over the blackness of his coat.

She had slept soundly all night while he lay restless and had scarcely wakened this morning to his kiss when he left her. And he felt desperately that she would never tell him anything, and he must find out how to make her tell him, and so he had put the letter in his pocket to read it again, to study its every word, not to show it to Sara. And now suddenly he wanted Sara to know everything about him, how he had ever come to marry Louise.

Sara put the letter down. She must not speak the anger she felt against another woman, though her blood ran hot through her body.

"Perhaps I married Louise too quickly," Gray said humbly. "Perhaps she didn't understand just what our life is here. She thought the Orient must be romantic and full of that damned charm everybody talks about. She didn't expect it to be what it is—work and sickness and poverty and filth and crowds and all this bombing going on."

133

"It is much more than that," Sara said.

"Yes, but that's all she sees," he groaned. He thought of telling Sara about the little Chinese child, and then could not. He did not want to think about it. There were perfectly good people who didn't care about children. It occurred to him at this moment for the first time that sometimes when he had talked about their having children, Louise had said nothing. He had talked on and on, a fool for children, taking it for granted that she would want them too.

"She has nothing to do," Sara said suddenly. She folded the letter and handed it back to him.

"God, she hasn't, has she!" he cried.

"I should think any life would be dull if you had nothing to do," Sara said. "I will not defend her," she thought passionately. "It would be too much to ask of me that I defend her." And yet she loved this man far too deeply to hurt him through his wife.

"I believe you've found the trouble," he said. His heart leaped to excuse Louise. "Of course you have," he went on. "She's used to something going on every minute—you know what New York is."

"No, I don't," Sara said quietly. "I grew up on a Kansas farm, and I've had to work ever since I can remember."

"Well, there was a lot going on in Louise's life," he said, "and of course spending hours in a bomb shelter gets monotonous."

"Yes," Sara agreed in the same quiet voice. "People

134

don't seem to realize that war is fairly monotonous to most of the people involved." She stopped herself there. She must not say what her mind ran on to think, "But how could there be anything but excitement and joy in being married to you, Gray?"

Each was silent for a moment. Separately they were making up their minds to the same thing.

"I shall have it all out with Louise tonight," Gray was thinking.

"I'm going over there my first free moment," Sara was thinking fiercely. "I don't care if she does hate me for it. She hates me anyway."

"Thanks, Sara," Gray said. He tore the letter into pieces and threw them into her wastebasket. "You always help me."

"I always want to, Gray."

They smiled quickly and parted. The moment he was gone she drew her day's schedule toward her. At ten o'clock she had an appendectomy. There should be plenty of time, barring complications, for her to go to see Louise at noon. Gray would be safe until one o'clock. They were never away from the hospital together in these times, and hers was the hour between twelve and one.

. . . All morning she planned what to say to Louise, and yet at twelve when she sat in the living room she did not know what she could say when Louise came in. Siao Fah had jerked his head at the bedroom door.

"She still sleeps," he said. "I will wake her."

She had been about to say, "Let her sleep," and then did not. She had so little time. "It is important," she said instead.

Siao Fah had given an enormous thump on the door. "She will come out," he said, and went back to his kitchen.

And a moment later Louise had put out her blonde head. "Oh, it's you," she said sleepily.

"I'm sorry, I have to see you," Sara said.

"I'll be out in a moment," Louise said. She shut the door, and Sara sat waiting, looking about the room. It was almost exactly as she had made it. Louise had put scarcely a touch upon it. A gold cigarette case lay on a table, an extra cushion was on the couch. Sara felt her heart a throbbing lump in her side. "I'm scared," she thought in amazed self-disgust. Why did a selfish little woman have the power to terrify her?

"I must forget she is Gray's wife," she thought, and knew it was impossible. She never saw Louise or spoke to her without thinking, "This is his wife—this is his wife."

And when in a little while Louise came in, her fair hair damp and curling from her bath, her little body wrapped in creamy satin and her bare feet in satin mules, it was idle, it was folly, to think she could forget for a second that this small, exquisite creature was Gray's wife. Beside her Sara felt large and plain and work-a-day. Of course any man would love this little pretty thing instead of a woman who had no time from morning to night to brush her hair or to look in a mirror. No, she thought honestly, it was deeper than a mere question of time. It was the sort of woman she was. Even if she were not a doctor in a Chinese hospital and a war going on, she would probably forget to brush her hair or powder her nose. There would always be something else. But whether Gray loved her or not, she loved Gray; and if Gray wanted Louise, then Louise must love him. She would pretend nothing except her purpose. She began it simply and directly, as she began anything hard and that she hated to do.

"Gray and I have worked together a long time," she said. "It'll be three years next July."

Louise stared at her, astonished, and did not answer.

"You'll wonder why I've come. It's because I know what a fine doctor he is after all that time. But he's a great deal more than a doctor. He's a human being, and he's a better doctor if he's a happy human being. He isn't happy now."

Between Louise's long black lashes her golden eyes began to smolder. Still she did not speak. Sara went on:

"You are his happiness, you know. There is only his work and you. He loves his work and you—nothing else."

Louise wrapped her robe about her more closely, tucked her feet under her on the couch, and lit a cigarette and blew its smoke from between her pretty lips.

"Do you think it possible you only imagine Gray isn't happy?" she asked. Her voice was so sweet that Sara's heart shivered. Louise looked thoughtfully at her cigarette. "Perhaps it is you who are not happy," she said. She shook back her fluff of hair and smiled. "Poor Sara!" she said distinctly, and thus with so few words opened to the cruel light of her amber eyes Sara's shivering heart. And now she gazed full at it, still smiling.

Sara felt herself ready to flee. She had held her secret as her treasure, never to be uncovered. And now Louise had uncovered it by a few ruthless words and by the gaze of those ruthless beautiful eyes. Then she rose to battle.

"Don't pity me," she said clearly. "Pity Gray. The only tragic thing in the world is to discover that what one loves is too small. That tragedy I shall never know."

"There," she thought in calm triumph. "Let that suffice."

Louise's eyebrows lifted, but her eyes fell. Sara considered those dark lashes. Should she mention the letter or not? She decided not. She went on, "Why should I tell you what you know already, since you chose to marry Gray? I have never known a man fit to stand near him. I only hope, for myself, that I can be half as good a colleague in the hospital as he deserves. I am only anxious that nothing"—she paused for emphasis upon the word—"that *nothing* will make him unhappy, no uncertainty anywhere in his life, no lack of loyalty or appreciation from us all."

Louise rose. "Are you trying to tell me something?" she inquired.

Sara leaped up. "Yes! That I hear things about you that I should not hear! And if I hear them, Gray must hear them."

Louise gasped. "Why—why—of all the impudent—"

"See to yourself, then," Sara said sternly. She turned and went out of the room and out of the house. What good had she done, she thought, except to make it now impossible ever to be near Louise again, and so separate herself still further from Gray?

"But perhaps it will bring her back to him," she thought. She paused in the February sunshine and gazed at a la-mei tree, whose golden buds were opening cups of fragrance upon bare brown branches. Lao Wang had planted the la-mei for spring and fragrance. Standing there she drew in deep breaths of that sweetest scent, to excuse her agony. But in a few moments she went on again. She had a shrapnel case waiting for her at one o'clock.

. . . In the room Sara had just left Louise walked about in impatient anger edged with fear. What did the woman mean? How much was truth, and how much

139

jealousy and frustration? Of course, Sara was mad with envy of her. Sara was foolish about Gray. Louise frowned. It was certainly not good for Gray to have a silly woman at hand constantly adoring him as he worked, even if he did not care for her.

"We've got to get away from this ridiculous place," Louise thought. She sat down again on the couch and piled the pillows about her and lay so still for so long that Little Pig opened the door to peep at her.

"Get out!" Louise said, and he shut the door in terror.

But she went on thinking long after that, smoking one cigarette after another, and every now and again flinging back her flying hair. How much did Sara know? What had she heard? But if she herself told Gray everything, explained to him that she wrote the letters because she had to, because she could not endure another raid? And she could say, couldn't she, that everyone else was spared too? She could make it sound all right, because Gray loved her so much. She got up at last.

"I rather think I'll be sweet to him," she thought.

She crushed her cigarette, yawned, and sauntered into the bedroom and began to brush her pretty hair with long slow strokes, calculated to make it shine.

. . . "I do want a baby, darling," Louise murmured. It was night, she was safe, and she laid her head upon Gray's knee. Under the Chinese lamplight her hair shone like carded silk before it is spun.

She spoke out of the silence when on the couch before the fire Gray after dinner had sat thinking how to begin, and she had wondered only when to say what she planned to say.

His astonished face looked down into hers, and he was stricken with tenderness. "Louise!" he whispered. "Why, darling!" He gathered her into his arms, against his shoulder. All that he had thought of saying fell into fragments, and he threw them away.

"I've been thinking and thinking," she said restlessly. "I know you haven't been quite happy, darling—" She paused. Did he or did he not know Sara had come over to see her? Better take the chance, even though it was not necessary! "I didn't need to have Sara come over and talk to me, darling. I knew, by myself, that I haven't been nice to you lately—"

"Sara?" he inquired. "Did she come over here?"

"This morning," Louise said, pouting. She lifted her little pointed finger and traced the outline of his lips. "She thinks I don't love you enough. But I love you all I have, Gray. Maybe it's true I'm not big enough for you."

"Did Sara say that?"

"Yes, she did, Gray, and I cried like anything afterward. I know I'm not good enough for you, Gray. I wish I were big and strong and capable, darling. But I'm not. I'm just—me."

"I only want you," he said, and would have been angry

with Sara in his heart except that he knew she had come only to help him.

"Of course I know she's in love with you," Louise was saying, "but so am I, Gray—terribly. That's what she can't realize."

"She's not in love with me, dearest."

"Yes, she is, Gray."

"I don't want to know it, then."

"No, Gray. Don't let's think about her—only you and me. Gray!"

"Yes, darling?"

"I *have* been unhappy."

He sighed. "I'm afraid you have, sweetheart."

"But it hasn't been just because of me. It's been because I haven't known how to go on with what we want. I do want a baby, Gray. But how can we have it here? It wouldn't be right—all the bombing!"

He did not answer. He sat slipping his fingers in and out of her hair as it spread from her face. Such a lovely, lovely face, he thought, so perfect in its every line, so childlike in its delicacy! This was what had been the matter, then, this was what made her so restless. She had felt frustrated about having a child, and so with that irresponsible quality which was one of her charms, she had turned to other things, her little dinner parties, even her friendship with Harry. She was trying to fill her life in ways that she knew.

"Perhaps it wouldn't be right to have a baby just now,"

he admitted. "But the war can't last forever—and it makes a great difference to me to know you want my baby, Louise." His voice was shy.

"Of course I do, Gray," she said. The light fell into the depths of her earnest golden eyes. "You couldn't take me away, could you, Gray, so we could—have one right away?"

"No, darling," he said. "I can't leave now."

She did not answer. When she did it was by the smallest of sighs and a question. "Gray!"

"Yes, dear?"

"Sometimes I wish— Is there anything I could do at the hospital?"

He answered her with deeper tenderness. "Why don't you come over tomorrow and see, darling?"

"Would you like it, Gray?"

"Love it!"

"It wouldn't bother you to have me around?"

"I'd like you right under my feet." He lifted her to him, and under his kisses she murmured in mischief:

"But Sara will be cross."

"Eh?" Gray paused.

"I said, Sara won't like it, if I am in the hospital!"

"Hang Sara," Gray answered.

"If you like," she said with laughter and triumph.

She was so pretty, he thought with quivering tenderness—but why did Chung bring her letters? The sharp question clung in his mind like a dart thrown into flesh.

He would not pluck it out. If he did, the wound might bleed. And if she loved him—and would she want his child if she did not love him?

At the keyhole Siao Fah put his eye on a level with Little Pig's. When he saw what was going on he said severely, "Do not corrupt yourself with such sights." He whacked Little Pig on the cheek with the wire egg beater and stuffed the keyhole with the end of a dish towel.

VI

Louise tripped up the hospital steps with her little high heels clacking. The hospital was quite quiet and clean, for almost no one was here. Perversely, she thought, the Chen-li people had stopped coming now that it was really safe to come. She pushed open the swinging doors, guarding carefully her bouquet of Chinese lilies.

Gray, hearing the light clatter of her footfall, opened his door and saw her coming down the corridor, her blue dress clear color for her glowing face, and for a moment he put aside again his question of her, never answered because love kept it unasked. How pretty she was, how sweet and suitable it was that she should bring flowers to his hospital! How impossible that she could be anything except what she looked! He had simply said gruffly to Sara the next day, "We were wrong about Louise—both of us," without having the courage to tell her that he had never asked Louise about the letter. "I'm glad, Gray," Sara had said quietly. Since then Sara had avoided him, but it was easier if she did.

Now Louise was at his side.

"Who is the lucky one this morning?" he asked playfully.

"Whom do you say?" she asked, smiling at the adoration in his eyes.

"There's not much choice—the hospital is so empty," he said ruefully. "One of the hospital orderlies broke his arm yesterday. There are a few people in the charity ward. And, of course, Yasuda's still here. I can't get at his trouble. Chung's making fresh tests today. It's almost like a typical case of sleeping sickness, the man's half-conscious so much of the time."

"Shall I give my flowers to Yasuda?" she asked. She had been on her way to Yasuda, anyway, but her eyes were innocent beneath Gray's.

"You may find him unconscious now." He hesitated, then he glanced about the empty hall, then tipped up her chin with his forefinger and kissed her. "It's lovely to see you coming in with flowers every day for somebody, my beautiful," he said.

Down the hall Sara's door closed softly. She had been about to come out of her office; but now, seeing the kiss, she stepped back and stood, her hand on the door, her lips pressed together. She was frightened at herself. When in her life before had she hated anyone as she hated Louise? When, indeed, had she ever been so angry with anyone as she was with Gray? How could he be so fooled by this silly flower stuff? Whatever had been wrong, Louise had got him back again. She groaned at herself, bewildered with her own contradictions.

"But that was what I wanted, wasn't it?" she thought.

Surely to have Louise love Gray was what she wanted? Surely she had answered honestly to him that day, "I'm glad, Gray." But she had not been near to him again. They had come and gone in the quiet hospital, making work where there was none these days, and he came late and went home early.

She waited a moment more and opened the door. The hall was empty now, and she stood irresolute. Where had she been about to go? It was no longer important. She went slowly upstairs to her own rooms. Her little Chinese baby was there playing on the rug. An amah sat near, sewing. The baby could sit up alone, and now when she saw Sara she smiled and put up her arms and Sara took her and sat down and held her.

"I'll take care of her awhile," she said to the amah, and when the woman gathered her sewing and went away she was glad to be alone. This little creature, she thought, looking at the baby, was going to be very pretty. She had the doll-like look of all Chinese babies, and the tiny hands fumbling at the buttons on Sara's uniform were exquisite as flowers. And then quietly and to the child's wonder she began to weep. For a long time they sat thus, she weeping and the child watching. Then she wiped her eyes. What was the good of weeping when nothing could be done? For the first time since she began to love Gray she wished she could go away, go somewhere far enough so that she and Gray could never meet. "If he's really happy with her, I never want to see him again!" she thought passionately, and then to her shame she sobbed aloud and went on sobbing and could not stop. And the baby looked frightened for a moment and then accepted the strange noise and tried again to pick off the bright buttons.

. . . Yasuda was not asleep. He was never asleep when Louise came in with her flowers, but she had not told Gray, nor had she told him that she came in almost every day now because she liked Yasuda. He was courteous and dignified, and he never mentioned the letters. Instead, when she stayed a few moments he talked of Japan. This morning when she came in he smiled and in his careful English said at once:

"I was thinking of those very lilies this morning. It is the season for them in Japan too."

"I caught your thoughts, then," Louise said, smiling. "The lilies grow on the south side of our house, and I picked them for you." She filled a green bowl with water from the ewer.

"In Japan," Yasuda said gently, "every house has the flowers blooming now. My people love flowers."

"I hope I can go there sometime," she told him.

"You will go," Yasuda replied, "and you will like my

people and they will like you. Let us hope for the war to end soon. Ah, how I hate war! Let us hope for swift victory and so for swift peace."

Then she heard him call her name.

"Mrs. Thomison!"

"Yes?" She turned, smiling.

"Let me say something long in my heart." His voice was clear, his words distinct. He was very conscious now.

"What is it?"

"Be sure, when peace comes, that my people will not forget what you have done for me. There will be a reward for you."

She felt elated as she heard these words and actually a little excited. She smiled at the pale dignified face upon the pillow.

"Thank you," she said simply.

And a few moments later, her flowers arranged, she tripped through the halls again and thought, "I really do like Mr. Yasuda, and I can't believe all the things Gray says about the Japanese." She made up her mind as she stepped out into the warm spring sunshine that she would talk with Harry Delafield about the Japanese when he came to tea next time. He had lived in Japan before he came here.

Someone passed her; it was the pretty Chinese doctor. Louise smiled at her brilliantly, but the girl did not smile back. She looked stern and preoccupied, and Louise shrugged and went on.

. . . Upstairs in her little living room Sara stopped her tears suddenly and rose. Siu-mei was at the door. She had come for her daily meeting with her lover. Months ago Sara had given this room impulsively one day for such meeting, and now she wished she had not, because the more she saw of Chung, the less she liked him. He grew very arrogant, as though he were sure of some power of his own. Today he came late again to meet Siu-mei, and, Sara thought, to avoid herself. But still, this might be her own sad imagination and she told herself that if Siu-mei loved this man, what right had she to hate him?

She went away with the baby with no more greeting to Siu-mei than a quick smile, and in her bedroom sat doing nothing as she watched the child at play upon her bed. She was glad Siu-mei had been too absorbed to see her face—though Siu-mei saw very little these days! The girl was really in love with the handsome young Chinese. Siu-mei, always so disciplined to calm, could change into a blushing child under Chung's eyes. She sighed and sat listlessly idle. She was very tired, though she had not known it until today when she saw Gray kiss Louise. Now nothing seemed worth doing.

And then suddenly in the silence she heard voices quarreling. Could it be Siu-mei was quarreling with her lover? She tried not to hear, but the rapid interrupting voices told their own story clearly. They were quarreling!

Then she heard Chung's quick step and the sound of a door shut. She opened her own door and saw Siu-mei sitting there alone, her cheeks very pink.

Sara came into the room. "What is wrong?" she asked.

"Chung says Chen-ta, the Eagle, has been defeated at Sian-chow. I told him I would not believe it," Siu-mei replied shortly.

"It is very bad news, certainly," Sara said gravely. "The people of Chen-li put all their trust in Chen-ta!"

"Chung says it is the beginning of many defeats," Siu-mei said with anger in her voice.

"And you?" Sara asked.

"I—I do not agree with him!" Siu-mei cried. "I say anyone can be defeated once. It means nothing." She sat silent for a moment, brooding.

Sara looked tenderly at the beautiful girl. "Do you really love Chung?" she inquired.

But the question was too frank even for Siu-mei's anger with her lover. She turned her face away and would not answer for a moment. Then she rose and leaned toward Sara's ear.

"Yes!" she whispered shyly, and went away.

. . . The quarrel went on between Siu-mei and Chung when, four days later, Chen-ta was again defeated at Pao-shan.

"What did I tell you?" Chung asked her. "Chen-ta is

a peasant and the sons of peasants his soldiers. How can they withstand a modern army? The country is lost unless we have something better."

"You talk and do nothing!" Siu-mei cried at him.

"What can I do except what I do—my work?" he replied. Then he grew alarmed at her anger. After all, what was Chen-ta to them? "Let us forget this thing, my Siu-mei," he said.

But she only said, "How can I forget that the enemy will descend upon us if Chen-ta does not hold them back?" And to his warmth she could answer nothing but sighs, and at last he grew angry and left her again because she could not put aside Chen-ta.

He could not tell her, of course, that she need not fear whether Chen-ta were defeated or not. He himself would be safe even if the Japanese marched into the city as long as Yasuda was his friend. And he would keep Siu-mei safe, naturally, and all her family. His plans were very clear. When the enemy was about to take the city he would urge the white people to escape. He would be nothing but courteous, but he would insist on their going. They could trust him, he would tell them. He would take care of the hospital. When the Japanese took the city, he was to be made governor of the province. Yasuda had promised him this.

The third defeat of Chen-ta was a week later at Liu-an-fu. Only by miracle was that defeat accomplished, for a letter which Chung had taken to Louise—he called her "Louise" in contemptuous secret—had somehow not reached the hand for which it was meant. He discovered this by chance through his brother, who came to tell him in the night that Chen-ta was preparing to march southeast the next day.

"But is he not to attack Wu-shan?" Chung inquired in great anxiety.

"No, we march instead against the garrison at Liu-an-fu," Chung Third said. "The Eagle has changed his mind because of his two defeats." He saw his elder brother's frown and said pathetically, "My life grows very hard for me now. The Eagle changes his mind often. We prepare to march south, and instead at the last moment we march east. Or we are told to face west, and then we are turned north. And somehow I must slip out of the ranks and come to tell you."

"You must indeed," Chung said fiercely.

"But do I not deserve a little more reward for it?" Chung Third pleaded.

Chung turned his back on him. "When my plans have been fulfilled it will be time to talk of reward," he said coldly, dismissing his younger brother.

Chung Third went away seemingly humble but filled with a hatred against his brother so great that he scarcely noticed a girl who stood near the door when he opened it. She was a pale, pock-marked girl who was not worth notice. But there she was. If he had waited he might have seen her stand for a moment there before Chung's door in the dimly lit corridor, and then turn the handle of the door softly and go into his room. But he hurried on his way and saw nothing.

The girl was Ya-ching, and she had put her ear to the keyhole and heard seven words out of ten of what had been said between Chung and his younger brother, and then she guessed at all she had not heard. In the hunger of her unreturned love for Chung, she came often to his door at night to listen, to watch. She could not believe that Chung and Siu-mei did not meet alone here. When the old barriers between man and woman broke, she told herself, so that they looked at each other and talked together, were not all barriers gone? And if she found it true that Siu-mei came to Chung's room at night, it would be a weapon in her hand to be used secretly or openly. Tonight she had found, not this weapon but another. She saw a man go into Chung's room and come out again. She had listened and heard enough for her use, and she decided to use it quickly while the blade was hot and new.

She stepped now into Chung's room so silently that she had to cough before he heard her. He sat by his table writing a letter, and when she coughed he leaped and put his hand over what he wrote as he turned.

"Why are you here?" he demanded when he saw her.

"I heard," she said simply.

"You will ruin your good name if you stay here," he said.

"I heard," she repeated.

"Heard what?" He set his white teeth together as he spoke.

"I know what you are doing," she said.

He leaped to his feet. "Leave my room!" he shouted.

But she did not fear even his anger if it only brought her his notice. "I will not tell anyone," she said softly. "Do you think I would harm you? I came in only to say—use me if you need someone to serve you faithfully."

As for him, he now heard her urgent voice for the first time. It might be well, he thought, to have a faithful woman, ready to obey his every command. It might be well to secure her to him. If only her face were not ugly or he were not fastidious!

"How can you help me?" he asked.

Then she turned her head away, and in the lamplight he saw the curve of her shoulder and the outline of her slender waist and hip. She had taken off her uniform and put on a deep red robe of silk—for him, he knew. It was a pretty garment. He glanced and saw its long narrow skirt was cut as the fashion was to show her ankle and leg above the knee. It was a slender ankle, and there was a graceful shape above it. He had often heard that women with plain faces had bodies most beautiful.

"Use me as you will!" she whispered. She drooped before him, and he felt a power rise in him over this helpless woman who offered him herself. He liked power over anyone. The room was still, the house silent, and it was midnight. Who would know what happened in this room? He took one step to the door and locked it.

"Do you know what you do?" he asked her. His eyelids thickened slightly as he looked at her, and his lips changed.

"Yes," she said, and did not turn her head. And she thought, "If the whole pomegranate is not to be had, is a part not better than none?"

. . . When Chen-ta's fourth defeat came to pass, Siu-mei said nothing to Chung nor Chung to her when the news came. But nonetheless she did not like his pleasure in his own rightness when they met that day in Sara's room. She thought for the first time, "Can it be he wishes the enemy to win?" She cast away the thought instantly, but not quickly enough to escape her own alarm. Then she strengthened herself by asking questions to her own scorn. Why should he wish the Japanese to come to Chen-li? Would he not suffer as they all would? Could any possible good come to him from being a traitor? And then when she had let this one word "traitor" come clear into her mind she cast it out quickly. How could she think that word when she looked at her lover, as she now did, and saw him young and handsome, a man of talent and education and all that young men craved to be these days? In instant remorse she put out a tender little hand to him as he sat beside her on Sara's couch and said:

"I wish one thing—that you would not seem so friendly with the sick Japanese. Why do you not let his case be taken care of by Thomison doctor?" The rumors in the city had reached her ears long before today, that the hospital was safe because it sheltered a Japanese officer.

"Yasuda?" Chung inquired, surprised. "But I am interested in his case—a peculiar case with which I am experimenting with a new drug. Now I suspect a tumor on the brain."

"He will not soon be well, then?" she asked, very troubled.

"Not soon," Chung said calmly. He had not taken the little hand on his knee. He would not, he decided, until he need not defend himself. There was no urgency in him to take her hand. Ya-ching, whom he did not love, had nevertheless drained him of urgency. It was true, as he had suspected, that her body was beautiful. And in the night it is easy not to see a face.

"Do you know that we are losing patients because of this Japanese?" Siu-mei said. "Do you know that people are saying now that we are safe in every raid because we are friends of the Japanese?"

"What does it matter what common people say?" he answered. And then after a moment he said one more thing, "It may be well, one day, to have been friendly with those who may conquer."

This he said to begin to make her ready, but he himself was not ready for what she now did. For she leaped to her feet and bent over him, her eyes sparkling and flashing, and that tender little hand which had lain upon his knee was lifted and laid so suddenly and sharply across his cheek that the sting of it brought tears to his eyes.

"You speak as a traitor might speak!" she cried, and like a whirlwind she rushed out of the room. And Sara came in early that day and she found him with his eyes watering and his handkerchief to his cheek.

"A lover's quarrel," he said, to her astonishment, and went away, a smile on his face that he dropped as he crossed her threshold.

. . . The city of Chen-li was dark with gloom under the cloudless sky of the clear winter's day. The gloom had nothing to do with the air raids, which the people now took as a matter of course when the weather was fine. Air raids they had learned how to live with, as they had learned in other times to live with pestilences and famines. For Buddha had given them the rocks in which to hide. The great cliffs behind Chen-li had been placed there, they believed, against this day. There was an old Christian or two among the refugees, and they sang a song of peculiar meaning. It went like this, "Rock of Ages, cleft for me, Let me hide myself in Thee." Every pagan in Chen-li now knew the meaning of this foreign song. "Doubtless the foreigners began singing it," the old Christians said, "out of just such necessity as ours."

It was not air raid, therefore, that cast them down this day. No, they were cast down because it was now rumored everywhere in the city that the Japanese, for some secret reason of their own, did not wish to bomb the hospital. Why? Because, reasonably, a Japanese lay ill there. But why was a Japanese there at all? Did it not mean that the American doctors were his friends? And if they were his friends, then they were enemies of the people of Chen-li. All their good deeds of the past were as nothing if now they befriended a Japanese. This had been a slow-gathering gloom in Chen-li, and the fruit of it was at last that very few people went to the hospital for any cause. At first some people had made haste to take shelter there when it appeared the Japanese would not attack the compound. But if there were a Japanese inside, then certainly it was right to be safe. They began to avoid such safety.

This gloom now grew desperate for another cause— Chen-ta, the Eagle, whose ragged guerrillas had won every battle against the Japanese before, now suddenly began to be steadily defeated. There were no newspapers in Chen-li, but none were needed. Lips whispered and ears heard, and thus mouth to ear over the whole countryside and through the gates into the city everyone knew how things were as soon as they had happened.

Thus on the third day of the last month of the year the flying word said, "Chen-ta has been defeated a fourth time at San Wan-tse." Now, San Wan-tse was less than fifty miles away. Even if there were no roads for automobiles, the enemy could proceed at ten miles a day if they were not stopped. So far they had always been stopped. But now what had happened? Ear to mouth heard that the enemy, who had always been surprised easily in the strange terrain, was now somehow always prepared; and when they were prepared they could resist, for their weapons were too good. Chen-ta's men, daring and impetuous with anger though they were, could not penetrate the solid wall of Japanese firing their big guns. The best that Chen-ta could give his men were odds and ends of guns and old rifles he had picked up when he could. The only good weapons he had were what he had taken from the Japanese. Now he had been repulsed in four attacks, and everybody knew that this could not go on. His own men would turn against him if he were not soon victorious again.

The people of Chen-li talked and took counsel, and they sent six of their most respected citizens to inquire of Chen-ta what he would do. Chief among these men was Mr. Ling, Siu-mei's father. He had not wanted to go because the only means of travel was by wheelbarrow over cobbled country roads to the mountains, and then by sedan chairs that bearers swung on their shoulders along the edge of cliffs. But the people of Chen-li compelled him by appealing to his honor as a chief citizen, and then Siu-mei had compelled him.

For Siu-mei had gone straight to her father's house from her quarrel with her lover.

"You must go, father," she said. "You must find out the truth. Our only hope is in the Eagle." She had not forgotten Chen-ta's bold and rugged face. It was clear now in her mind as she spoke.

"I suppose I must go," her father said, sighing. He roused himself to smile at her ruefully. "How peaceful would man be without woman!" he remarked.

"So peaceful you would not be alive at all," she retorted, and they parted laughing.

Thus Chen-ta in his mountain garrison a few days after this received the six elders of Chen-li. They came windblown and somewhat terrified, though trying not to show it, after the journey along the tops of cliffs. The garrison was in a lonely temple up against the sky. Chen-ta had seized it for his own, though he let the three ancient priests who were there stay on and dust the gods at New Year's and pray their prayers, and they were well pleased because he fed them with his hordes and spared them the trouble of going out with begging bowls. When they missed their old quiet peace in the midst of all the noisy, scuffling young men, they remembered how full their bellies were and let what was go on. Their only trouble now was to resist the meats that those men loved, and their chief prayers were for strength to eat only cabbage when the smell of pork was in their nostrils. They fell into this sin sometimes and climbed out again with groans and fears of hell after all their saintly years.

These three old priests now met the elders as they came on foot up the last rocky steps which even the bearers could not climb with burdens on them.

"Is this the revered nest of the great Eagle?" Mr. Ling inquired.

"It is," the eldest priest replied.

"Let him know that six men of Chen-li await his word," Mr. Ling said.

They had all stood facing the gate while they waited lest, turning, they must look down the steep rocks up which they had come and must go down again. But they had not to wait too long. The gate opened, and a guard stood there and bade them enter and led them to the main hall where, below the great Buddha, Chen-ta was waiting. Mr. Ling, weary as he was, saw that even the high gilded Buddha did not dwarf the tall young man who stood at its feet. It seemed rather to retreat into the shadows, waiting and protecting.

"Seat yourselves, old sirs," Chen-ta said calmly. He waited until they were seated, and then he sat down too. They waited while he sent for tea and sweetmeats, and they heard him order a meal for them of the best the mountain had.

"Do not trouble yourself," they murmured.

"It is my pleasure," he replied.

And so, when they were rested a little, Mr. Ling began, since it was agreed he must be spokesman, and in winding, devious, courteous words which seemed all praise, he made known the purpose of this visit from the Chen-li elders. Out of all the praise Chen-ta plucked the question.

"You come to ask why I am defeated," he said bluntly.

They coughed politely, and each sipped his tea. This was assent.

"I do not know," Chen-ta said in the same bold, frank voice. "If I did, would I let defeat go on? All that I can say is that, whereas before the enemy was always surprised when I came, now he is always ready."

The old men looked at each other.

"There is a spy," Mr. Ling said gently.

"There has never been a spy among my men," Chen-ta said proudly.

No one contradicted him. No one spoke for so long that Mr. Ling knew it was his duty to speak again.

"When the enemy is a common one," he said in a judicial voice, "then we may proceed in common ways of war. But this enemy is no common one. And we must therefore expect uncommon things."

"If there is a spy among my men, he sleeps dead tonight," Chen-ta cried passionately.

"When a man feels a flea bite," Mr. Ling said again, "he finds the flea before he kills it."

163

Chen-ta laughed suddenly. He liked this old man with the long, sheeplike face and little fringy beard.

"I will find my flea, old sir, if he lives," he cried cheerfully. He slapped his knees. "What is your honored surname?" he inquired.

"Miserably, it is Ling," Mr. Ling replied.

"Ling?" Chen-ta repeated. "I met a Ling doctor at the hospital where my prisoner lies."

"That was my negligible daughter," Mr. Ling said proudly.

How could old Mr. Ling now understand the new attentions which Chen-ta urged upon him? He pressed every dainty upon him and deferred to all his ideas for searching out spies, and at the feast which was spread in the second hall of the temple before the figure of the God of Wealth, which was made almost as big as the Buddha, Chen-ta put old Mr. Ling in the seat of honor and drank empty to him innumerable small cups of wine.

It was night before Mr. Ling caught a glint of light from the meaning of all this. He only of the six elders had been given a room alone. The old priests had been turned out for this, though he did not know it. He lay upon a priest's hard bamboo bed, fearing he had eaten and drunk too well and that he could not sleep. Then into the lonely room Chen-ta came. The old man started up in his bed in confusion, but the young man pushed him down by the shoulders and sat down beside him.

164

"Do not rise," he said. "I came only to ask a question. I am a common man and one without grace. What I say, I say as a beast makes its cry, knowing no other way to speak. Is your daughter betrothed?"

And Mr. Ling gasped and blinked. This was directness indeed. He felt as though snow had fallen upon him.

"Yes," he stuttered, "ye-yes, by her own choice."

Chen-ta's face set itself. He was silent a moment.

"By her own choice?" he repeated.

"She is very modern," old Mr. Ling said apologetically.

"Who is the man?" Chen-ta demanded.

"A doctor, Chung by surname," Mr. Ling replied, not sure whether he should give any man's name into such keeping.

"That mutton-face!" Chen-ta cried.

Mr. Ling smiled but did not speak.

Chen-ta sat frowning. "I suppose your daughter does not even remember me," he said moodily.

"Yes, she does," Mr. Ling said eagerly. "In fact, it is due to her that I am here. She insisted that I come. She said, 'Our only hope is in the Eagle.'"

"Did she say that?" Chen-ta asked sternly.

"As I am here, she did," Mr. Ling said solemnly.

The moonlight shone clearly into the room, for the paper was torn out of the ancient lattices and none had replaced it. Chen-ta rose and went over to the lattices and threw them open. Then he stood, very straight and bold in the brightness of the night. A faint distant roar floated in upon the wind. It was scarcely more than the noise an insect makes with its wings.

"The planes are over Chen-li," he exclaimed.

Mr. Ling clambered out of bed and went to see for himself.

"So they are," he said. They could see the darting flashes pale in the moonlight.

"Is she safe?" Chen-ta asked in a low voice.

"Perfectly," Mr. Ling said. "Strangely enough, the hospital has not been hit in months. All the city is talking evil of it. They say the Japanese are protecting it."

"What?" Chen-ta shouted. He seized the old man's shoulder. "I have not been told of this!"

"You have not come near for a long time," Mr. Ling said.

"No, because my messenger I sent there always told me that the Japanese was worse," Chen-ta exclaimed.

"Your messenger!" Mr. Ling repeated. "Who is he?"

"A common fellow," Chen-ta said. Both minds were working now with each other.

"Why did you choose him?" Mr. Ling inquired.

"He said he knew the way, having gone there once to have a wen cured on his cheek."

"Is he loyal?"

"He came to me as a deserter from the government troops."

"A deserter," Mr. Ling mused.

166

"But for a good reason," Chen-ta said quickly. "He would not join in their retreat."

"A reason good, if true," Mr. Ling said, and sneezed in the wind.

Chen-ta let his hand drop. "Get back to bed," he said. "It would be poor thanks to your daughter to let you fall ill in my camp." He helped the old man back and spread the padded quilt over him. Then he stood for a moment. "We may catch a flea," he said.

"It may be," Mr. Ling agreed.

"Good night," Chen-ta said. "We meet again to-morrow."

"Tomorrow," Mr. Ling echoed. He waited until the young man was at the door. Then he called, "There is one more thing."

"What is it?" Chen-ta asked, his hand on the wooden latch.

"As to my daughter," he said and paused. In the moonlight he saw the young man suddenly motionless. He went on, "I would like you to know that her choice is not mine."

The young man now coughed in his turn. "As for me," he said, "I should like you to know that your daughter is right—about me, that is. I go on to victory."

He marched out and shut the door softly behind him.

. . . In the city, at that moment, under the darting, forking, twisting lights of falling bombs, the hospital stood quiet, an island of peace. Gray did not rise from his bed. Louise did not even wake. But Sara was always restless now in moonlight, and she got up and put on her robe and soft Chinese slippers and walked noiselessly about the hospital, from floor to floor, making sure that no one was frightened. She hesitated a moment at the corridor to the men's ward and then went in. There was no use in waking Dr. Chung. She would just see for herself that all was well. An orderly nodded in his seat, but she let him sleep. The hospital was, for the first time in the years that she had known it, more than half empty. The people of the city had turned against it. Who could have believed that to be safe was to be accursed?

And then in the midst of the darkness she saw a crack of light under a door. It was Yasuda's door. She paused, uncertain whether she should go in. But if the man were ill? She listened and heard voices so soft that she could scarcely be sure she heard them in the roar of dull distant explosions. Then she was sure. She threw the door open suddenly and saw Yasuda sitting up in his bed, Yasuda who for days had lain half-conscious in the strange coma that no one could explain. Beside him sat Chung. Between them lay a map. They stared at her, transfixed.

VII

SARA, looking at the two men, did not let her eyes waver.

"You are better, Mr. Yasuda," she said distinctly.

"Much better, I thank you," Mr. Yasuda replied. He folded the map carefully as he spoke.

Chung rose. "What you have said is most interesting," he remarked to Yasuda. Then he turned to Sara, his teeth very white through his smile. "Mr. Yasuda has been showing me a terrain map of the central provinces which the enemy used in their march west. Very clever!"

Sara did not answer the smile. "When did this remarkable change occur in the patient?" she asked.

Chung picked up a chart from the small table by the bed. "Mr. Yasuda has had no fever today. In fact, his temperature has been dropping for thirty-six hours. He enjoyed his noon meal, he tells me."

"Very much," Yasuda murmured. The map was now in a small square, and from under his mattress he pulled out a flat leather case and put the map inside it. Then he lay back against his pillows and gazed at Sara between his lids. His pale face was blank. But so was Chung's also. These two faces now confronted Sara with a look so alike that for the first time an enormous possibility dawned in her mind. There was an evil connection between them. She had come upon some hidden, electric cord of communication. She suddenly felt frightened and helpless. Yasuda—perhaps he was not ill at all! He did not even look ill now. She was alone with these two men.

"I am sorry if I interrupted you," she stammered and, turning so quickly that she stopped herself lest it seem flight, she left the room and went back along the corridors and up the stairs to her room. She must tell Gray as soon as it was morning. Twice she was sure she heard a footfall behind her, but she would not turn her head to see if Chung were following her. If it was he, then she must keep steadily on.

When she reached her room she hesitated for one moment, and in that moment she turned her head and saw not Chung, but the nurse Ya-ching watching her. Ya-ching had followed her, not Chung!

"What are you doing here, Ya-ching?" she called angrily.

"I came merely to see if Ling doctor's light was on," Ya-ching said. "If it was I was going to ask her a question about a certain thing. But her transom is dark, and I will wait until tomorrow."

The girl disappeared as she spoke. Sara waited a moment more, hesitating whether or not to call Siu-mei. She decided she would not. She had nothing to tell her except an intuition of evil. Siu-mei was in love with Chung.

"I must tell Gray first," she thought. "Gray will know what to do."

. . . In her bed Siu-mei, whom the distant bomb had not wakened, now felt herself drawn out of sleep by a touch upon her outflung arm. She sighed, dreamed for an instant of her lover, and then woke, startled by the dream. He could not be here in her room! But they had quarreled about that only the other day, because he did not want to meet her in Sara's rooms any more.

"You are so old-fashioned," he had said, shrugging his handsome shoulders.

"Then I will be old-fashioned," she had replied proudly.

She opened her eyes and saw, not Chung, but a girl, standing in the shadowy darkness of the room.

"Ya-ching!" she cried.

"It is I," Ya-ching whispered. "I am in great trouble, Ling doctor."

Siu-mei sat up and put out her hand for the light, but Ya-ching stopped her.

"Let me speak in the darkness, Ling doctor." She knelt beside the bed and began to sob softly.

"Don't cry," Siu-mei said, astonished. "Speak—tell me what is wrong." She had never liked Ya-ching and blamed herself, thinking that it was because Ya-ching was so ugly, and for this reason now she was gentle. The girl came of mean birth, and this meanness showed in her looks and behavior; but for this, too, she could not be blamed.

"I cannot find words to tell you," Ya-ching said in a small voice.

"Is your family in trouble?" Siu-mei asked to help her. "Has your house been bombed?"

Ya-ching shook her head. "No, it is I, myself."

Siu-mei put aside her first quick guess. There were many young girls in trouble these days, when all the usual ways of life were disturbed and changed, and war gave strange freedoms between men and women. But surely a girl with a face like Ya-ching's was safe?

"Are you ill?" she asked.

"Yes," Ya-ching said desperately. "I am sick with shame. I have no husband, but I am with child. Cure me!" Ya-ching besought her eagerly. "Give me a foreign drug!"

For a moment Siu-mei did not reply. But why, she inquired of herself, should she be filled with loathing for Ya-ching? A common girl had fallen into a common plight. As a nurse Ya-ching would have to be dismissed, but still helped somehow as a woman.

"I cannot," she said at last sternly. "It is not allowed.

I should forfeit all my years of work here if it were discovered I did such a thing."

"Then I will kill myself," Ya-ching said passionately.

"That you may not, either," Siu-mei said at once. "Consider reason. What you have done is a pity. But there are ways. Will the man not marry you?"

"Shall I tell him you say he ought to marry me?" Ya-ching asked. She lifted her head.

"Yes, certainly tell him so," Siu-mei said with earnestness. Some orderly, doubtless—there were several young orderlies. "And say that I will be your go-between, so all may be done decently and quickly."

For answer Ya-ching buried her head again in the silk quilt. Her shoulders shook and she made small stifled cries. She was sobbing, Siu-mei thought, and listened again. No, this strange, ugly girl, she was not weeping —she was laughing!

She shook Ya-ching sharply. "Why do you laugh?" she cried.

And still Ya-ching would not answer. Instead she leaped to her feet and ran from the room, her cloth-shod feet silent, but the sound of her stifled laughter breaking the sudden silence of the night.

And left alone in her room Siu-mei listened. The air raid was over. She had scarcely noticed it, so used had she grown to safety. And yet now she felt no longer safe.

And Ya-ching ran creeping along the dark corridors

of the almost empty hospital, guiding herself by her hand on the walls. No one was there to see her. Not even an orderly sat in the hall now. There was no need. She went down the stairs and up again into the men's hospital to Chung's rooms. The door was locked, but she had a key of her own, and she fitted it to the keyhole and went in without a shred of noise.

Chung was there, poring over a piece of paper with a small magnifying glass. He put the glass down as she came in, and he looked up.

"Go away," he said, "I don't want you here tonight. I have work to do."

She stood before him, not moving. "I will not go until you have heard me," she replied.

"What do you want?" His hand holding the microscope was poised for her going.

"I am in trouble," she said.

He took up the paper again and began to study it as though she were not there.

"Will you not ask me what trouble?" she inquired of him.

"No," he said distinctly.

She flew at him then as any common angry woman flies at the man who stirs her to fury. She seized him by his ears, and she screamed at him.

"You shall hear me—you shall know—"

Then he struck her full in the mouth, and his hand,

soft and smooth, was suddenly hard. She staggered and put her hand to her bleeding lips.

"Your trouble is none of my business," he said. He took out his silk handkerchief and wrapped it about his hand as he spoke. "I care nothing about any trouble of yours. You may be ill, you may be about to die, and I do not care."

"My trouble is worse than that," she faltered.

He looked at her, his eyes wide as a tiger's eyes. "Still I do not care!" he shouted.

And then she knew that he knew what her trouble was, and that it was true that whatever it was he did not care. And he saw that she knew.

"I let you come here," he said contemptuously. "I never asked you to come. Now I tell you, do not come again!"

And then she cried out indeed, for she still loved him and would always love him in her stupid, desperate way, knowing she was never to have anything from him except what she had already had. She ran to his feet and fell there.

"Do not say never!" she cried weeping. She caught his foot in her arms. "I will not complain. I take back to myself all I said—it is my trouble, it is not you who is to blame—it is all I—if only I may come here sometimes, when you say I may, only—"

"I have said—never!" Chung broke in, and when she clung to him, he dragged her still clinging to his foot across the floor, and at the door he lifted his free foot and pushed her out into the hall, and he took from the keyhole the key he had given her, and he shut the door and locked her out.

And she lay there sobbing and no one heard her in the empty hospital. And after a long time she went creeping back to her own bed and lay there and wept until her tears were dry, and then she lay there, plotting through the night until dawn. One by one she drew out her weapons and surveyed them in her mind. There were the pills that she had taken that night from Yasuda's bed. She had them still, and she had seen Chung making the same pills. There was the man creeping to his rooms. She would wait for that man and force him to talk. And she would tell Siu-mei who it was that should marry her and would not. Slowly through the hours her love for this man grew evil as a poison in her, and with all her wild love turned an agony in her she swore herself against him whom she loved, and she was ready to die if she could only see him die first.

. . . Two days later Chung Third, coming to the hospital, felt himself seized by the sleeve outside the gate. It was dark, and he was instantly afraid. He went afraid all the time now because Chen-ta was behaving so strangely that no one knew what he was going to do next. He ordered all his troops one way and yet willfully at the last moment, at a moment now twice when Chung Third had already slipped out of the ranks, Chen-ta changed all he had planned. When Chung Third returned to find his company, none were there. Only by much questioning of the farmers and passers-by could he discover where Chen-ta was, and each time Chen-ta had seen that he was not where he should have been. He had had to find quick lies to save himself. Once he had said, "I misheard, Great One. I thought we were told to go south."

"It is strange that, out of all my men, only you misheard," Chen-ta had said.

Chung Third had not dared to let his eyes slip from the strong black gaze that held them.

"I am only a common useless fellow," he had stammered. "What I do is of no account to anyone."

"You are too humble for yourself," the Eagle had replied with strange emphasis.

So the next time Chung Third had tried to make a joke of it. When the Eagle sent for him to know why again he had been left behind, he made a noise as like laughter as he could under the Eagle's terrible eyes.

"Great One, I saw a pretty woman last night—a willing-looking woman. Sir, I am a poor weak small man, so I gave in to her. You, sir, would not understand, but there are many like me." He made a noise like laughter again, but the Eagle stayed grave.

"If this happens once more, I will say there is one too many like you," he said distinctly.

"It shall not happen again," Chung Third had stammered. "Sir, I swear, however willing the women are I will look straight ahead."

"See that it is so," the Eagle had replied.

But Chung Third had gone out of that presence trembling like a bamboo leaf in a typhoon. He was, he felt, a mere nothing between these two strong ones, the Eagle and his own elder brother. But he feared the Eagle more, and so he had determined with much groaning to go to his brother's once more and tell him where the Eagle would strike and then tell him that he was watched and could come no more. Now that he was near the hospital he felt himself so afraid that he was not sure if after all he did not fear his brother as much as the Eagle. It was at this moment that he had felt his sleeve taken.

"Let me go!" he squeaked like a rat, and darting and turning he tried to break free.

But the hand twisted itself into a knot in his sleeve, and a light flashed upon his face.

"Be quiet!" He heard a woman's voice and was so astonished that he stood still. A woman! He felt less afraid. What could a woman do to him?

"You go to Chung doctor?"

In the reflected glow of the flashlight he saw her face. It was the ugly girl he had seen that night outside his brother's room. Fear went out of him.

"Why should I say I do or do not?" he retorted impudently. He jerked his arm suddenly, but her grip still held.

"You are the one I saw before," she said. She flashed her light up and down the street. No one was near. She let the light go out and they stood in darkness.

"What if I am?" he retorted.

"Are you his friend or his enemy?" she asked.

Chung Third grinned into the night. "Neither—I am his brother."

She was struck silent by this. Chung's brother! She had not dreamed of it. Then he might be coming merely with family news. Yet if that were so—

"Why do you come in the night?" she asked.

"Because he bids me not come by day," Chung Third replied.

She thought desperately, "How can I bribe him to truth? With what can I pay him?"

"Are you younger or elder than your brother?" she asked.

"Younger."

She hoped a little again. If this was a younger brother, he would have reason to hate Chung. She made a great guess.

"The evil your brother does is known," she whispered. "I came to warn you."

Chung Third felt his sweat start. "Why warn me?" he faltered.

"Because—because why should an innocent man suffer with an evil one?" she replied.

"I am innocent, truly," he groaned.

"So, I came to tell you," she whispered. "Do not go near him tonight. You may be seized when he is seized."

"But—but I have something to tell him," Chung Third stammered. "I came all this way to tell him."

"Is it written down?"

"No, it is only in my mind."

"Then tell me, and I will tell him," she said.

Now Chung Third was divided against himself. He longed to tell her and be spared meeting his brother— and what if she spoke the truth? Besides, if he got away as early as this he might return to his place before the Eagle missed him. And yet, who was this woman?

"How do I know who you are?" he asked.

"Tell me what is in your mind," she said. "Tell me, for I know already what your brother is doing. Why should you die with him?"

Her voice in the night was terrifying to him, it was so strong, so willful. He was afraid of women. Though he talked much of them among his fellows, he was frightened and silly when one spoke to him. Besides, did he not fear the Eagle more than his brother? The words he was holding in his mind burst out of him like firecrackers.

"Sha-wu mountains, tell my elder brother. Tell him just those three words. And tell him the first night of the new moon, and tell him that I do not know when I can come again. That is all." He gave one great wrench and left a piece of his cotton sleeve in her hand and ran through the dark streets like a fleeing dog.

And she threw down the rag and then picked it up again and rolled it into a ball in her hand and went creeping back through the gate she had left unbolted. She had all her weapons ready now.

. . . Sara, looking out of her window the next morning, saw Gray already out in his garden. She had not slept—had he, too, not slept? She stood, her silk robe clutched about her, her long hair down her back, and watched him. It was spring again, the lovely Chinese spring, so early green with willows, so early flowering with pear and plum blossoms. Gray was planting something in a little flower bed at the side of the steps. She saw him stoop for a moment and dig with a short-handled Chinese spade. The early sunshine struck his face, half turned toward her, and she saw it clearly. Then he turned his face, she thought, toward her, as though he felt her gaze. No, he was not looking at her. He was lifting his face to the sky, weighing, she knew, the day. Was it clear? Would it be a good day for flying? She could catch his question. So, too, did she question the sky each morning. He searched for a moment the cloud-lessness of heaven, and then she could all but hear him sigh as he went back to his work. And stopping often to watch that tall figure bent over its labor, she washed and dressed herself, content creeping into her in spite of all. For he was there and she was here, and the same wall encircled them, and was not that much for content? In a world so large he might have been somewhere and she here, and the wall between them. Whatever was, they were within call, within speech, within daily meeting. And today she would have to talk long with him, for she must tell him of Yasuda immediately.

A little later in her living room she touched a bell when she had finished breakfast, and when the amah appeared she said:

"Tell Thomison doctor that when he has eaten I should like to talk with him over a matter," she said.

"So," the old woman muttered and trotted away.

She watched the amah approach Gray and give her message and saw Gray rise and dust the earth from his hands, and to her surprise saw him come at once. She ran downstairs to meet him at her office door.

He came in, his eyes very clear, the breath of morning fresh upon him.

"But have you had your breakfast?" she cried.

"Long ago," he said. "I couldn't sleep."

"Nor I," she said quickly. "The strangest thing, Gray —I hardly know how to tell you." And then she did tell him, wondering if she had made too much of that scene in the night. He would be impatient with her and call her feminine and prone to imagination.

But now he only listened to her gravely, his eyes fixed on hers.

"That is very serious," he said when she had finished. "Certainly it is very serious. I don't like it at all." He sat frowning and thinking. This was the second inexplicable thing about Chung. This morning, alone at breakfast, he had asked Siao Fah suddenly:

"Does the mistress still have the letters from Chung doctor?"

He had asked Siao Fah against his own will, and yet he had had to know. And Siao Fah had answered steadily, "He brings them as he always did."

And then Gray had not been able to swallow another mouthful. He had flung down his napkin and had gone outdoors to work furiously in the garden, and when Sara's old woman had come he had followed her without going in to wake Louise with his kiss, as he always did every other morning. He felt very far from Louise these days. His love was quivering and wounded. What did she hide, he asked himself, when he saw her bringing in her flowers to the hospital, when he saw her about his house, when she lay in his arms? Why did she not speak? But she did not.

Now here was Chung, looking at a map with the Japanese. A sinister business, if one believed in the sinister. But he did not. There was always a reasonable explanation to everything. If he could ever bring himself

183

to ask Louise, he would probably find it was all nothing —the letters. Delafield had been to the house at least twice since the night of the dinner, each time gay toward Louise and friendly to him. There was nothing to make anyone think—he frowned again and tried to fasten his mind upon this matter of Yasuda and Chung.

"I had better just go straight to Chung," he said. "It's my instinct to drag things out into the open. I'll just tell him you told me and ask him about it." He paused, thinking. But if he did that, how could he keep from asking Chung about the letters? And he would ask no one of his own wife. Louise must tell him herself. He would not spy on her through another. "I'll just have a look at Yasuda first," he said. "If Yasuda is himself, I can get at it through him."

"That might be well," Sara said. "Shall I come with you?"

"Yes," he said.

Together they went to Yasuda's room. The door was opened to their knock by the nurse Ya-ching. She stood there in her clean blue uniform, her pale pocked face expressionless.

"How is he?" Gray asked.

Ya-ching gave her little ducking bow. "Thomison doctor, he is as always."

"You mean he is unconscious again?" Sara demanded.

"If you speak loudly he can hear," Ya-ching replied.

They went to the bed quickly. There Yasuda lay, his

184

face upturned, his eyes half-closed, his hands limply turned palms upward at his side.

Gray took his wrists. "Pulse weak," he said after a moment. "Respiration not at all what it should be," he said a moment later. He lifted Yasuda's eyelids. "Look at this!" he bade Sara. She looked and saw Yasuda's eyes. They were petrified and unseeing, the balls turned down until only a rim of black showed in the white. Gray turned suddenly on Ya-ching.

"Was he like this all night?"

"All night," Ya-ching said.

"But I saw him myself in the night," Sara cried, "and he was not like this."

"I saw him only like this," Ya-ching insisted.

"But you were not here all night," Sara said.

"It is true that for a little while Chung doctor stayed here and sent me away," Ya-ching replied.

"I came in then," Sara told her, "and he was not like this."

Ya-ching's face did not change. "As to that, I do not know," she said. "I do not know what he is when I am not here."

Not to these two would she give her weapons, she was thinking. She would use them first on Siu-mei. This morning she had seen the one last thing needed to whet her determination to its final height. She had seen Siu-mei and Chung meet upon the stairs, the one coming down and the other coming up, and she herself looking down on both from above. And she had seen them hesitate for a moment, and then Chung had taken Siu-mei into his arms. Only for a moment it was, but it was eternity for her, watching from above. It was only a moment, and Chung had gone on down and Siu-mei had run upstairs, her face rosy and smiling, and that beautiful smiling face had been the last thing needful for Ya-ching. She had wanted to scream and shriek, and then she remembered her weapons. She could sever those two clean, one from the other, and she would.

Under the eyes of the two Americans she kept her face empty. They turned from it to look at each other.

"We had better talk this over before I see Chung," Gray said. He strode out of the room, and Sara followed him. "Come to my office," he told her over his shoulder. She went down the hall behind him. A siren shrieked for an air raid, but neither of them heeded it. There was something closer to them, more terrifying to them than airplanes. There was something here in the hospital, some alien enemy thing. And Gray, walking down the corridors to his office, was cutting away from himself everything except the cold determination to discover it. Whatever it cost him, he would know. He shut the door behind Sara and turned the key in the lock.

"Sit down," he commanded her. And then he sat down behind his desk and, facing her across it, he told her.

"Sara, Chung is still bringing those letters to Louise." And when she leaned forward, her face instantly intent, he said, "What has Louise to do with Chung? When I find that out, I'll have the truth."

He tore Louise out of the shelter of his heart with those words and held her there to examine as he might examine anyone in this office. "I've got to stop shielding her," he muttered and would not look at Sara. "I've got to know—not for my sake, but for the sake of—the hospital."

The long wail of the siren went on and they waited for it. Soon from where she sat facing the wide window and the rocky hills she would see the long wavering line of people climbing to their caves again. Chen-li was nearly all in ruins now. The packed houses of the city, centuries old, had fallen like children's blocks beneath the bombs, and acres of blazing fires had crumbled wooden pillars and beams. But the people came out of their caves and searched the ashes with their bare hands and rescued fragments of goods and furniture and in the ruins opened their little shops again to sell a few loaves, a handful of cake, a half-dozen cans of American milk, a basket of damaged oranges, and from the country farmers brought their vegetables and fruits every day and from the river the fishermen their fish, and they stuck their flags into piles of broken brick and cried their wares until the air-raid warning came yet again.

Sara's eyes filled with tears suddenly, and Gray saw and was shaken to the bottom of his being. He had often seen Louise cry. Her pretty eyes filled easily, and he had come now to realize that those tears lay just under her eyelids, very close to the surface, very ready for her use. Last night she had been angry with Siao Fah for disobedience. His mind flashed back over the tempestuous little scene, so like many another. She had ordered roast duck for dinner, and Siao Fah had bought pheasant again, because, he said when Gray sternly questioned him, he knew his master liked pheasant better than duck.

Gray had laughed. "You oughtn't to mind that," he had said to Louise.

But Louise had flown into inexplicable anger, had leaped up and run from the room, and when he followed her she was crying. He had taken her in his arms.

"You always side with Siao Fah," she had sobbed on his breast.

"No, I don't, darling," he had said humbly. "But why hurt his feelings when he is so faithful?"

"Faithful only to you!" she had cried in real fury. And then she had made her old complaint against him, her real complaint, the cry with which she carried on all their quarrels into one great quarrel. "You will do anything for a Chinese—you sacrifice everything to them, even me!" This was what lay between him and Louise, like a great and immovable stone. He had long ceased to give her any answer, and he gave her none last night. He had simply held her until she had stopped crying.

But never but once had he seen Sara cry.

"Sara, don't—" He stopped and turned his eyes away

from her quivering face. He had never seen her as anything but his comrade, steady and courageous and gay.

"Don't mind me," she said brokenly. "I'm not crying for any—particular reason. I mean, when I saw the people beginning to climb those hills again—I just began to cry, senselessly."

He wheeled his chair to face those hills, and they sat in silence watching. The second warning sounded, and the long thin blue line of people thickened. It was a glorious day, a warm swelling bursting sort of a day, when leaves were unfolding quickly and bamboo shoots pressing upward and blossoms opening in an hour or two. But the people were hurrying underground.

"Here we sit," she said fiercely, the tears running down her cheeks, "perfectly safe, perfectly helpless, not knowing what to do! After the raid is over the wounded will simply—lie in the ruins. They won't come to us. They'd rather die than come to us. Gray—I haven't dared to tell you. But two days ago I went out into the streets to—to them after the raid. I took some first-aid stuff."

"They wouldn't let you touch them," Gray broke in.

"How did you know?" She wiped her eyes.

"Because I've tried it myself," he said grimly.

It was true. Each alone had gone out, not able to bear the knowledge of suffering. And each had come back.

"Thank you, thank you," one after the other of the people had said. "We need nothing, we thank you." So even a dying man had spoken to Gray as he stood beside him and said with such dignity of death at hand that Gray had not been able to serve the man against his will, even against death.

"Gray, what shall we do?" Sara rose and came to his side and stood there, and he rose too and stood, and they watched the thing they had watched so often before. But this time it was new and terrible to them as it had never been before. They had no part in it. That was the horror of this moment. They were here and useless. Without their knowledge they had been made enemies of all that they loved.

The airplanes were thick in the sky now, coming in threes, in sixes and nines, over the old city. The bombs dropped, and bursts of fire followed quickly, like fountains of flame set free. Black clouds of smoke rolled out, and the sunlight dimmed. The hills were hidden, and they were in the midst of darkness divided by tongues of fire reaching into the sky.

Someone rattled the door and found it locked, but they paid no heed to it, and whoever it was went away again. Gray thought of Louise a quick moment, and as though she had caught his thought Sara said:

"You were speaking of Louise."

"Never mind," he answered. "It doesn't matter—nothing matters. Anyway, she's as safe—as we are."

What mattered in the world except what they now saw before them? For suddenly out of those rolling clouds three enemy planes appeared and above them one small Chinese plane. This small plane dove down beneath the large ones like an angry insect, and then flew upward. From its jaws they could see against the black clouds two tiny jets of fire. They were the two small machine guns which must fire upward into the belly of their prey to wound it.

"Sara, look!" Gray shouted. The small plane had darted up to entangle the very wings of its enemy, and they saw two planes out of the three falter and flutter downward. And then the smoke rolled over the incredible scene again and curtained it. And they turned to each other, gasping and laughing and sobbing and crying out broken words to each other.

"Gray, did you ever *see* such . . ."—"It's not to be believed—it's the sort of thing that makes you want to go out and tear yourself to pieces for them!"—"We've just *got* to . . ."—"You bet we will—nothing else will do—"

They seized each other in joy and exultation and suffering and wild worship for all that was brave and reckless and good, and in that great flood they flung themselves into each other's arms, forgetting their separate beings and made one by this joy which was bigger than they. She was in his arms, and her arms were about him and cheek was pressed to cheek while they cried out to each other. And then suddenly each was aware of the other. The world in the midst of which they had stood lost a second before ebbed away in great waves. They were themselves, alone, nothing around them.

She thought, "What I knew would never happen has happened!"

But he could not think. He could only feel her in his arms. Sara, the woman he had never thought of loving. But he did love her. Now he knew he loved her. Oh, all the trouble this was going to be! He groaned at the thought of it, the terrible, tangling trouble of it! But he could not let her go out of his arms. He had never felt such straight simple satisfaction in his life before as he did now, with her in his arms.

"This is going to be a lot of trouble," he muttered, staring down at her.

She looked up at him, her lovely face flushed, her eyes dark, her lips parted. "Let me go," she whispered.

But he could not. To have her in his arms was suddenly all he wanted in the world. "I can't," he said. And, seeing her lips for the first time in his life for what they were, he bent and kissed them.

And after a long time she said, "What are we going to do, Gray?"

And he said, "I don't know."

But he did not let her go, and she did not take her arms away from him.

VIII

Louise drew them apart. No one came to the door to open it, no voice called to startle them. But Louise came between them. Slowly Gray loosened the hold of his arms about Sara, and Sara felt them less close and for one fierce instant she tightened her own arm about Gray's shoulder. It was no use. Louise had come in through Gray's mind and memory. She was there as really as though she stood there staring at them. There was no denying her presence. So Sara, too, dropped her arms. She stepped back to lean against the desk with both hands behind her lest she fall. She felt numb and dazed except for the burn of her mouth. Her lips were stinging. She touched them with the tip of her tongue and looked at Gray. He looked at her, his dark eyes somber.

"It's too late," he said slowly.

"Nothing is too late, so long as we're both alive," she retorted.

He did not answer, and she saw that he was struggling

with the thought of Louise. He would have to tell Louise, of course. Deceit would be intolerable to him. She weighed her own conscience. It was as clear and light as sunshine. If Louise had really been able to love Gray, she thought, then she would have felt guilt. But Louise loved no one but herself. And to that self, Sara knew, she had done no hurt.

She cried out, "Whatever you decide to say to Louise, Gray, remember that I am glad that this happened. I shall always be glad. I can make it enough for my whole life, if it has to be—"

"Don't," he said, "it's not what we've just done. It's what it means—that we could do it at all."

"Simple and clear for me," she said. "I love you, that's all. And I'm glad. It's as simple as that for me."

"Have you—a long time?" His eyes were steady upon hers, but she could see the dark red stain under his skin.

"I don't know how long," she said.

She looked away from him. She was a woman naturally shy, and she had spoken with an honesty beyond herself. She could do it because in some deep hidden way she was fighting for her life against Louise. Yes, and for Gray's. "I can make him happy," she thought, "and Louise never can."

She gazed out of the window behind Gray. The flames were gone, and there remained only the rolling billows of black smoke. The room was full of the terrible silence that always follows an air raid. In that silence her voice sounded too loud, too bold, but what she had said was said. Nothing was hidden between them. She was bare before his eyes.

And he, looking at her, felt nothing done and nothing made clear. He was full of distress and tumult. What did it mean that he could kiss Sara and find in that one long kiss the deepest union he had ever known with another human being? But the kiss was not simply itself —it was full of the knowledge of Sara, of Sara working at his side at the operating table, Sara examining slides with him with eyes troubled in reluctant diagnosis, of Sara eager and quick in all their work together, forgetting herself to be his extra hands, his other brain, his eyes, and now his own heart.

He dropped into his chair, and leaned his head upon his hands, frightened at the terrible clarity of what he now perceived. Whatever he had given to Louise was not what bound him and Sara into one. He and Louise had never been one. There had been no knitting together of their separate beings. Marriage had not made them one. Nevertheless, there was marriage. Louise was his wife, not Sara. The fact rose before him, mountain high. What was to be done with it? Something must be done, for he could not live under the oppression of deceit or pretense of any kind. He sighed, thinking of Louise. Was he the dastardly sort of fellow who could get mixed up in his feelings with two women? He felt sick at the thought. What a hypocrite he was! Only this morning he had been blaming Louise because she had not spoken of her letters to Delafield, and now what he had done was infinitely more grave. The only thing he could do would be to tell her, to tell her at once. In the enormity of his dismay everything else seemed nothing —Chung, Yasuda, what now was anything when what he had to tell Louise was such disaster?

And all the time Sara stood at the window, waiting for him to speak. The quiet wind was moving the smoke solidly away now, and between the dark drifting pillars she could see the hillsides. The people were coming out of their caverns and down again to the ruined city to take up their lives again as best they could. They would search the ruins and the ashes for any scrap of something usable and with that take up their lives again, as they had so many times.

"And cannot I?" she thought. She felt the old rush of her love and admiration for them hot under her eyelids. Let Gray decide what he must do, she thought, and she could bear it somehow. Then he spoke.

"What shall we do, Sara?"

"Anything you think is best, Gray."

"No, not only what I think, Sara. How can I decide for—three?"

"Decide for two, that's all, Gray—you and Louise. I have decided for myself."

They looked at each other, honest eyes upon honest faces. Then he groaned.

"Why didn't I see it long ago—before I ever went away from you?"

She shook her head. The tears were suddenly thick in her throat, and she could not speak. She bent and kissed his hair and went quickly away. And he let her go, his question not answered. For who could answer it if he could not? And he could not. He only knew that he had been blind and now he could see. He sat there a long time, his head leaning upon his hands, thinking.

. . . Louise in her pretty living room was enjoying herself. Harry Delafield had come to tea. She felt it a small triumph, for he had put her off twice with pleas of unexpected work. She had been debating restlessly whether she would write him another note when this morning his own chit came asking if he could drop in this afternoon—he found himself unexpectedly free because a ship had been held up in the rapids and so he could not unload as he had thought he would have to do today. And she had scrawled on the bottom of his paper, "Do come, Harry dear. I'm lonesome." Of course it was not work, she had told herself resentfully. Men could always arrange their work when they wanted to, unless they had absurd consciences, as Gray had. But Harry had no such conscience, bless him! Now that Harry was here she had wholly forgiven him. He looked charming and debonair and gay when nobody else did. He enjoyed life even in such a hole as Chen-li.

197

He had come rather early, and they had sat through the raid feeling nearly perfectly safe and making signs to each other and laughing at the way they looked when they stopped their ears and hung their mouths open. Twice the bombs fell near enough to jar the house, and a teacup crashed to the floor. The raid was unusually short, but the sky grew dark with smoke and so she lighted the candles.

In the silences between the explosions they talked a little, watchful of the next thudding boom.

He said, "I say, it's very strange the hospital's never hit any more. It used to get hit such a lot."

She made a little face at him. "You know why it is— we have an important Japanese patient!"

"So I've heard," he said, and grinned at her daring. The booming began, and they hung their heads and covered their ears, eyes upon eyes. Then when there was silence again he said:

"I say, do you know the Jap?"

"You mean Yasuda?" she asked. "Yes, he's quite nice. I take him flowers."

"You're nervy, aren't you?" He was astonished.

"How?"

"The Chinese have it in for anybody who's nice to a Jap—you can't blame them."

She considered this a moment. "But the Japanese will win, won't they?"

He did not follow the circumlocution of her mind. "What's that got to do with it?" he asked.

"I mean—it doesn't matter what the Chinese think of one," she said.

"Oh, I see," he replied. "Well, the bets are all against China at the club down at the port. Still, one can't tell. The Chinese are so amazingly tough."

The booming began again, and now the room filled suddenly with red glare. They sprang up to go to the window and stood watching it.

"Lucky the wind's the other way," he said.

"They usually get the fires put out," she replied.

"Yes, and with buckets and little hand pumps," he said. "One has to admire them, you know."

But she did not answer this. They watched until the flames began to die down and only the black pillars of slowly swirling smoke remained, and then the quiet wind began pushing it away. They went back to their seats.

"I'm glad you're here," she said, smiling gently across the little fireside table. "I know we are safe here, but still I'm afraid."

"Then I'm glad I'm here," he said. He took the cup of tea from her and their hands touched and they smiled at each other again. He felt reckless today because he felt safe. He was going to be moved to a higher post. He had come especially to tell her and then had put it off because it was so pleasant to feel safe enough to make a little gay love to her. It was perfectly safe, since now he had his promotion and would be going away. He was glad he had not let himself fall in love with her, but still it was exciting to realize he actually did love her a little, enough to make him feel sentimental and sorry to think there would be no more of these times.

"You're looking prettier than ever, Louise," he said.

She flung back her bright hair. "I'm hideous," she declared. "What wouldn't I give for a few hours at Armand's on my hair and my skin! I'm a fright."

"A lovely fright," he said, laughing. He put out his hand and lifted the curling edge of her hair. It was soft, and he let it wind about his fingers, conscious of a certain teasing excitement in the act. Then she tossed her head and leaned back in her chair beyond his reach. But her amber eyes glowed at him from under her lashes. She would wait for his lead, she thought, smiling. She was so restless, so pent up in this little house, so bored in this ruined, stupid city that she would take any excitement. But she was not prepared for what he said suddenly after a moment.

"I say, Louise—I have to go away, you know."

She leaned forward. "Oh, why, Harry?" she said.

"Orders," he said. "I'm to be moved up a peg. It's a promotion."

He was elated to see the disappointment upon the pretty face. Since he was going away, why shouldn't they perhaps— The pretty face turned hard under his eyes.

"If you go, I'll simply die, I'll be so bored," she said bitterly.

He felt dashed. "I'm glad I've been of use," he said a trifle coldly.

She felt the coldness and put out her hand to him. "You've simply saved me," she said. "There hasn't been anyone I could—play with. I love so to play. I'm not a bit serious, Harry. I've always had a good time until I came here."

Something broke in two in him. One part thought, "Still, her husband's a decent sort"; the other smiled at Louise, comprehending her very well.

"I know—I rather like a good time myself," he said.

They sat measuring each other with their eyes. How far did play go?

"Where are you going?" she asked, delaying answer to that question.

"To Peking," he said, accepting the delay.

"Shall you mind being in Japanese territory?" she asked.

"Not a bit," he said. "What do I care? Besides, it'll be jolly getting out of raids."

"I wish I were going," she said.

"I wish you were," he replied. "Especially Peking. There's jolly riding there in the Western Hills. We could have some fun. I'll miss you, Louise."

"Will you truly, Harry?"

"Cross my heart."

Their hands clung together now, and neither pulled away.

"Do you know, Harry, I've often thought perhaps the Japanese weren't so bad as Gray thinks."

"Japan's rather decent," he admitted. "I've been there quite a lot."

"Have you? Do you think I'd like it?"

"I believe you would," he said. "Everything's small and pretty and frightfully clean—not a bit like China. It's all organized, like Germany."

"I was in Germany once," she said, "and I had such a good time. I liked the way the men clicked their heels and kissed my hand."

"Well, you always know where you are there," he said easily, "and it's just the same in Japan. Here, of course, it's every fellow as he's able. They're rather corking, though—take that guerrilla chap, the Eagle they call him—"

"I hate it here," she cried out. "I don't dare tell Gray how much I hate it!"

"It is rather rotten for foreign women," he agreed. But what he was thinking was whether or not he would kiss her. It had been fearfully long since he had kissed a white woman. He began to pull her toward him ever so gently. And she did not resist. Would there be any excitement in this, she wondered? Both of them forgot everything except this moment. He was on his feet now, and she rose gracefully to meet him, full of curiosity

Siao Fah, on his three-legged stool, his eye at the keyhole, choked, and when Little Pig came to ask him about the soup he gave him a push that sent him half across the kitchen floor.

"Don't ask me anything now!" he hissed without for an instant moving his eye. There was a long moment of intense concentration. Little Pig on the floor watched without daring to move. Then Siao Fah rose and dusted his hands.

"There," he said, "now I've seen it with my own eyes."

. . . Gray, coming in long after, found two quiet people by his fireside—Louise sat smoking one of Harry's English cigarettes, and Harry was smoking his pipe. The cold tea things were on the table between them.

He was so relieved to find Louise not alone that he did not notice the quality of the silence into which he entered.

"Hello, Delafield," he said. "Glad to see you. Louise, pour me some tea, please."

He sat down without bending, as he always did, to kiss her cheek. It would be absolutely impossible for him to touch her, he had decided.

"It's cold," she said. "I'll ring for hot."

She touched a small copper bell, and Siao Fah came in decorously quiet. "Hot tea," she said over her shoulder.

"I know," he said with dignity and in Chinese, taking up the pot.

"I was just telling—your wife," Harry said, not looking at Gray, as he knocked his pipe into an ash tray, "that I'm being sent up a peg."

"Not going away?" Gray asked.

"Yes—to Peking," Harry replied. He wanted Gray to know at once that he was going away.

"I'm sorry for that," Gray said. He tried to gather into focus his dazed thoughts. "I've wanted to tell you before how much I appreciate your making some fun for Louise," he said. "I'm afraid she'll miss you." But nothing he said seemed real. "So will I," he added. Still it was not real.

"I'll miss—this," Harry said indistinctly. He lit a fresh pipe and the smoke choked in his throat. "Dash it, the chap's too decent for me to carry on behind his back," he thought remorsefully. He rose, anxious to say his good-bys while Gray was in the room. Siao Fah came in with the tea.

"Oh, stay for a fresh cup!" Louise begged.

"Thanks, no—I must go," he said quickly.

"But we'll see you again?" Gray asked.

"Of course we will," Louise said. She pouted prettily, clinging a little to Harry's hand when he shook hers in his abrupt English fashion.

"Oh, yes—well, I hope so," Harry said. He drew his hand hastily from hers.

And a moment later he ran down the brick steps of the house and out to his waiting riksha, not knowing whether he was most glad or sorry to know he was gone for good. The moment when his lips had met Louise's soft mouth had been sweet, but not quite sweet enough to risk the hurt to that tall serious-faced husband of hers.

"Dash it," he thought again, staring at the smoking ruins around him without seeing them, "men have got to think of each other." He was relieved to discover that he was not really in love with Louise. Love was so complicating when one wanted other things more—success, for instance, in one's career.

By the time he reached his somewhat palatial and still-unruined bachelor quarters, the face he remembered most clearly was not Louise's but Gray's. Yes, he was very glad he was going. He would have been in a mess had he stayed.

. . . Siao Fah put on a clean gown of pale-blue cotton and washed his face. His master had eaten nothing of the dinner he had prepared and had sat, besides, looking white and tired. The woman was not worth it, but how to persuade him that she was not? This was what he was thinking passionately as he had passed soufflé.

"Serve your mistress first," Gray had said irritably. "How many times must I tell you?"

Unwillingly Siao Fah had obeyed. It was always intolerable to him not to have Gray's the first and best helping of that delicate dish whose perfection was his pride. But so it had to be. Then Gray had eaten nothing. And all through the dinner and the dishwashing Siao Fah went on making up his mind. After his work was done he would go over and see the woman doctor. Woman knew woman, and he knew there was no friendship between these two. The Durand woman doctor would know what to do if he told her what he had seen.

Thus at nine o'clock that night Sara heard a cough at her door and went to open it, and there was Siao Fah. She waited, thinking Gray had sent him with a message. But there was no message. Siao Fah merely said in Chinese, "I have a small matter."

"What is it?" she asked.

"I cannot speak it here," he replied.

He came in and shut the door carefully and then with whispering and mystery in his pocked face and in his gesturing hands he told her.

"I saw something today in Thomison doctor's home— while he was away!"

"Is it my affair?" Sara asked quietly.

"I ask your advice only," Siao Fah retorted. "Shall I tell him what I saw or not?" He paused, his face blank but triumph a glitter in his small black eyes. How could she advise if she did not know? She began, "How can I—" and he interrupted her swiftly.

"So I must tell you. This is what I saw: the Englishman and Thomison doctor's woman embraced. Then they put their faces together, mouth to mouth."

"Are you lying?" Sara's question was a cry.

"How can I think up for a lie that which I never saw done before by any human beings?" Siao Fah inquired.

He was not lying, that she knew. Oh, but who could tell Gray? Not she—not she! It was beneath her pride to use to her benefit a thing that Louise did. No, Gray must discover Louise for himself. She would not help him. She was what she was—he knew her well. She would take nothing from Louise to add to herself.

Siao Fah came a step nearer. "That is not all," he whispered. "The Thomison woman gets letters and sends letters. Chung doctor brings her letters."

In spite of herself she cried out, "Chung?"

"He," Siao Fah said solemnly.

"But why—" She checked herself. This was only a servant. But Chung—and Louise?

"When does Chung doctor bring letters?" she demanded. What Louise did was not her business, but what Chung did was.

"Every two or three days," Siao Fah said. He looked pleased. Ah, now she was beginning to believe him! He went on, "He gives her a piece of paper. This she reads. Then she writes on her own paper and puts a stamp on the envelope and I take it to the post office. I told you this before."

"Still does this happen?" she asked.

"Still it does," he replied. He leaned forward. "Once I took one of these letters, not to the post office, but to Thomison doctor, and he read it. But what can he do with his woman? She is like a fox, that woman! As soon as she talks he listens and believes her. So still there are the letters."

"But what—"

Siao Fah shrugged and coughed behind his hand. "What does she say? How do I know what a woman says? I have never demeaned myself to listen to one." It occurred to him that now he was talking to a woman, and he excused himself hastily. "You, Durand doctor, are not a woman. You are only a doctor."

A wistful pang shot through her. "Perhaps you are right," she said humbly. Out of the mouths of fools and sucklings, she thought—then she put herself away. Chung and Yasuda, Chung and letters—links were coming together into a strange chain in her mind. But Louise?

She inquired of Siao Fah, "Is there anything else you have to say?"

He scratched his head. "Is that not a great deal?" he asked.

"A great deal, perhaps, and perhaps—nothing," she retorted. She motioned Siao Fah away, and he opened the door and slipped through it like a shadow.

Alone in her room she went to bed but not to sleep. In the intense silence of the night she lay, thinking and thinking of Louise. What had Louise to do with Chung? She had never seen them even speak to each other. Yet they had spoken often. And what had Chung to do with Yasuda beyond what he should have as a doctor? Her mind refused the absurd possibility of intrigue. And yet there was this strange safety in which they lived these horrible days. Yasuda and safety, safety perhaps because of Yasuda? She had heard the rumors among the Chinese and had rejected them. But now, link upon link, the chain in her mind grew longer. All possibilities— nothing proved, she told herself strongly. She had an accursed imagination that loved to run ahead. She must not run after it. Let her wait and see. Wait she must, for to whom could she talk? Not Gray, if Louise were a link in that chain, not Siu-mei, who loved Chung!

"I wish I could get hold of that Eagle, Chen-ta," she thought suddenly. "I'd get him to take Yasuda away. Then we'd see."

The more she thought of it the more she wanted the thing done. If Yasuda went, whatever had been built upon his presence would tumble. Thought hardened to determination, and with determination she drifted toward sleep. Across that drifting she heard out of the night's silence the cry of a woman's voice in the street calling the soul of her dying child to come home, come home.

"Oh, the poor mother!" she sighed, and slept, as the voice died in the distance.

. . . "Gray is jealous," Louise told herself a dozen times through that long evening. "And frightened, maybe," she added, watching him. Why else was he irritable and then humbly sorry and eager to make amends?

"Don't mind anything I say or do," he told her brusquely after dinner. "I have one of those heads of mine." He stretched himself on the sofa and closed his eyes.

"Poor Gray," she said gently. She lay back in her chair, living over again the afternoon. Perhaps, after all, she was a little in love with Harry? Or was it only that she wished she were going away, too, and so with him? She sat up after long brooding over this. No, what she wanted, what she must have, was to get away from this fearful hole into which her life had fallen. It was absurd for a young and beautiful American woman to be locked up in a ruined Chinese town. It was not enough simply not to be bombed. There was more to life than mere physical safety. If Gray would go with her, well enough. Honestly, that would be best. But if he would not, she must go alone.

"Gray!" she said.

"Yes?" He did not open his eyes.

"Gray, let's get out!"

"Get out?" he repeated. He opened his eyes now to stare at her.

"Yes. I'm just—fed up. I—I can't stay any longer,

Gray." Her cheeks began to burn. "I hate this place so. I hate everything here. I try not to say anything, but I can't go on forever—like this."

"Is it because Delafield is going, Louise?"

His voice was so gentle that she was confounded and could not answer. So he went on, "Tell me, Louise. I think I could understand that."

"No—no, it isn't," she said then. "At least, truly I don't think it is, Gray. Perhaps his going makes me want all the more to—go—home, but—but not with him, if that's what you mean, Gray."

"I've thought for a long time perhaps you did—like each other," he said in the same tired gentle voice. "I never told you that Siao Fah brought me a letter once that you'd written to Delafield. I didn't want to read it —then I did. I had to. Then I told Sara—"

"You told Sara!" she cried.

"I had to, again," he said steadily.

"That explains everything!" she said furiously. "Her coming here to accuse me that day—her saying I didn't appreciate you. You should have come to me, Gray. I'd have told you the truth. Harry has given me some fun, that's all. He's made this place a little less dreary. That's all."

"That night," Gray said steadily, "I came in ready to speak to you, and then that was the night you said you wanted a child. Nothing else seemed important after that. It would have been an insult then to speak of the letter. I threw it away."

So that, she thought, explained the mystery of the lost letter! Chung had come to her angry and disturbed over it. The guerrillas had surprised a Japanese garrison because the letter had not reached the person it was meant for, he told her. She felt herself tangled in intrigue. But she had not planned intrigue—only some sort of escape from bombing, and those horrible hours in the shelter among disgusting people. Intrigue frightened her. She must, she must get away! Gray was saying something.

"Then you said you couldn't have a child here in Chen-li. You wouldn't, that is. It wasn't right."

"No, I won't," she said sharply.

"But recently I've been thinking, would you anywhere? Wasn't it just another—plan to get away?" He blurted this out, miserably conscious of his own secret. He had never had a secret in his life before, and he could not bear it now. Either he must tell Louise tonight, or he must go away from Sara and have no secret. As soon as he could he must make up his mind what was right for them all—not just for him. He was not free.

"No, it wasn't," Louise said. "How beastly you are, Gray!"

She took a cigarette and began to smoke in little quick puffs. "Gray, I'll show you if you let me. Let's go home to New York. We'll have a real house, a home, and a baby. I do want it so." She was quivering as she spoke. She did want it. Anything, anything to get away! She had come to wish—time and again she now wished that she had never married Gray. If she had married Jack or Lewis—they were both doing so well, her mother wrote. Jack had settled down to spending his fortune quite decently after his father died, and Lewis was a bank president now. She was actually jealous of their wives, living comfortably in the world to which she belonged. She looked about the room with such hatred that she wondered the walls did not fall away from her. Outside a dog howled, and then she heard a common sound of the Chen-li night, a mother calling the soul of her dying child, "Come back, dear one, come back!"

Over and over the melancholy voice cried on and then it faded into the distance of the streets. They sat silent, listening and not hearing. Then Gray said heavily, not looking at her, his hand shading his eyes:

"Louise, if you are sure that you want that more than anything in the world, I will go with you." For if she really did, he told himself, what right had he to refuse it to her, having promised himself her husband? There was so much he could not blame her for—the misery of this war, the terrors of the city, this life behind walls, lonely in spite of all he could do for her. He had been foolish to think that love could be enough. Perhaps it never was. Perhaps what he and Sara had was more than love.

"I haven't been entirely fair to you," he said quietly. "I'll make it up to you—and go."

And she, hearing these words, leaped from her chair and ran over to him and flung herself upon him, crying and laughing together:

"Gray, do you mean—Gray, will you really? Oh, darling, darling, darling!"

He let her cry and laugh and fondle his hands and face, and then he said, "You do love me?"

"Oh, I *love* you!" she cried.

"If I—go," he said indistinctly, "you must—love me very much."

"Oh, I will!" she cried. She jumped up and whirled about the room laughing and dancing, and he lay watching her, his hand over his eyes again. Now that he made a decision, his mind was clearing. Sara would understand that he must give Louise her chance. He had to be fair to Louise first, or everything else would be wrong. If he and Sara should—think of each other first, his conscience would be forever gnawing at him. He'd have taken something for himself at the expense of another whom he had promised—to cherish. Sara would understand him. Sara was so strong. She would be patient with him, and bear it and go on with her work. Besides, no one, nothing, could take from them the knowledge of what was between them, which was so much more than love.

Under his hand he closed his eyes and saw Sara's face

as it had been this afternoon, upturned to his kiss—her brave and beautiful face!

. . . At the keyhole Siao Fah watched Louise with stupefaction. He had been prepared to enjoy seeing her at least beaten when Thomison doctor came home and saw that other man sitting in his own chair before the fireplace and with his wife. But no, it appeared there was to be no beating. Instead the woman had been promised something evidently—that is, bribed.

"I shall have to go back to my own village for peace," he thought disconsolately.

He got up, put his stool under the stove, spat in the sink, and went to bed.

IX

"GIVE ME the yellow pills," Yasuda said.

Ya-ching rose in her slow sleepy fashion. She seemed always to be aware of nothing, and Yasuda, after long watching of her, had come to believe that she was as stupid as she looked. Indeed, Chung had said she was. "Besides, she is in love with me," Chung had added, laughing. "She will do anything for me!"

Ya-ching poured tea into a bowl and handed it to Yasuda. Then she took a small brown bottle out of the table drawer and shook two pills into the palm of her hand.

"Not with your hand, filthy hag!" Yasuda screamed in quick rage. "How many times must I tell you?"

"Ah, I am so stupid," she murmured. She threw the pills into the wastebasket, for once regretting her stupidity. It had taken her some time and much care to make these pills which looked exactly like the real ones. One would have said flour and water could be mixed easily enough, but the yellow was a strange shade. She had had a hard time even with sulphur, and only at last had she found a harmless dye. Harmless it had to be, for Yasuda must not confuse her with a new illness.

She shook two more pills into a bowl and he swallowed them with tea. Though he was now so familiar with the effect of the depressant which Chung gave him he could never avoid a curious and hateful feeling of terror while he waited for it to begin. He glanced nervously about the room.

"I shall sleep," he told Ya-ching. "Open the window a little more." Soon the oppression in his chest would begin. "Where are my papers?" he asked next.

"Here—under your pillow," she replied.

She watched him closely, seeming to be indifferent to all he did. He composed himself and lay back on his pillows and closed his eyes. She thought, watching him, had he taken the real drug, he would now have been turning ashen, his nails blue. There was no change. He lay waiting. Then he opened his eyes.

"You may leave the room," he said suddenly. "I prefer to be alone while I sleep." He dreaded the last sinking into unconsciousness. He could never be quite sure that he did not speak. If he did, probably it was in his own tongue, but still he preferred to be alone. She moved slowly and heavily to the door. "But come back in an hour to see that all is well with me," he commanded her. He closed his eyes. "I will simply pretend I am going into ordinary sleep," he thought, strengthening himself.

"So," she agreed carelessly, and shut the door upon him.

In the corridor she quickened her flat-footed pace. She had an hour of her own. The question was, should she use it to tell Siu-mei now, or should she wait until after the hour and go in and prove for her own eyes that Yasuda was himself, and so that the pills that Chung gave him were a poison? She could not, however she thought about it, imagine why Yasuda would be willing to take a poison; but if he were, if it were a poison, then Chung had intention in it with Yasuda.

She skirted cautiously about the door of Siu-mei's small office. A very little would have put her off. Had a patient been there, had there been danger of Chung's passing—but Chung she knew had gone to a foreign hotel at the port for a feast. This was his free day. She had seen him go, as she saw and knew everything he did in one way and another. And there were no patients in the hospital except two beggars in the charity ward. She stood tiptoe and pressed her nose against the slightly frosted glass in the door of Siu-mei's office. By staring hard against the light of the window within, she could see Siu-mei's dim shape, alone. She opened the door and peered in. It was true—Siu-mei was alone. The thing was decided.

Siu-mei looked up and saw her standing, back against the door. "What is it, Ya-ching?" she asked. The girl had not come to her since the night she had come to tell of her trouble. She had thought of speaking to Chung of that night to ask his help for the girl and then had not. After all, it was Ya-ching's secret, and heavy enough for her to bear without others knowing of it yet.

Ya-ching came slowly to the desk without answering. She put her hand into her bosom, still without a word, and brought out two small folded squares of paper. Then she opened them. Her hands, Siu-mei noticed, were pretty pretty and quick, too. In an instant the papers were open. They contained the same thing, small round yellow pills.

"Why do you put these before me?" Siu-mei asked, astonished. Then she was astonished at Ya-ching's look. The round flat face was awake with inner excitement. The thick lips trembled.

"This—and this," Ya-ching muttered, pointing at the papers, "are not the same."

"They look the same," Siu-mei said clearly.

"I made these," Ya-ching said. She pointed to one paper. "He made those." She pointed to the other.

"What he?" Siu-mei asked.

"Chung doctor," Ya-ching said.

Foreboding fell upon Siu-mei but she pushed it away. "What of that?" she asked, feigning carelessness.

"These—his—he gives to the Japanese," Ya-ching said. "And then he always goes to sleep. Have you not seen how he sleeps? His body is half dead, and his breath stops and his eyes roll in."

"When? When does this happen?" Siu-mei asked sharply.

"Every day, at least once," Ya-ching replied.

"Why?"

"How do I know? A nurse is not told."

The two women looked at each other.

"How long has this gone on?" Siu-mei asked. She sat motionless, her two hands clenched. She was stiff with foreboding now. It was no longer to be pushed away by any strength she had.

"For months," Ya-ching replied.

"And you have said nothing!" Siu-mei cried. She leaped to her feet. Oh, she must find defense for him whom she loved! "You come to me now, ready with your accusations! I ask you—whom do you accuse?"

Ya-ching hesitated. She had thought she might not yet tell the whole. If she only told a part, that part with which she had nothing to do, if she told only enough to make him suffer, it might be enough revenge, and still in the future she might have some sort of confused hope. But hope for what? For now, as she stood thus face to face with Siu-mei, she saw how beautiful she was. Here was a face which, if a man had, he could want no other, those black eyes the shape of apricots, the moth eyebrows, this mouth red as a pomegranate—all the old phrases for woman's beauty crowded her mind as she saw them come true in Siu-mei's face. What folly any hope of hers!

"I accuse—the man who put this in me," she said, and pointed to her belly.

Siu-mei gasped out her relief. "Oh," she sighed. "Oh-oh, is that all! Oh, I was afraid, for a moment!"

"You were afraid it was Chung doctor," Ya-ching said in her harsh flat voice. "You are right—it is he."

She met Siu-mei's eyes, she waited in her speechless silence, while these words went home to Siu-mei's brain.

"I don't believe you," Siu-mei stammered. Her mouth was stiff, and she could not go on. Her tongue was too dry to wet her lips.

"It is he," Ya-ching said. "Why do I accuse him? Because he pushed me out of his door with his foot." Two yellowish tears gathered in her eyes, and she let them roll halfway down her round scarred cheeks. Then she took the edge of her white apron and wiped them off. She felt in her bosom again and brought out a scrap of faded blue cloth.

"Here is another thing," she said. "I tore this from the sleeve of his younger brother, who is a guerrilla in the Eagle's band. But this brother comes and goes with messages to his elder brother. From whom, I do not know. And why, I cannot tell you. But they are messages like this—'The Sha-wu mountains'!"

"How do you know this?" Siu-mei whispered.

"I saw him enter his elder brother's room one night," Ya-ching replied, "and so another night, not long since, I laid hold of him and frightened him. I told him the evil his elder brother did was known and he had better not come in lest he be caught in it. And so he gave me the message and escaped my hand. But I held his sleeve and tore this out of it."

Siu-mei could not speak. She sat staring at these things before her. And Ya-ching went on in the same dull and heavy voice:

"What one thing has to do with another, I do not know. I am not clever enough to know the meaning even of what I see." She paused and went on again. "There is a third thing. These," she pointed to one paper, "I gave the Japanese to eat today. Go in and see for yourself if he is well or ill. If he is well, then what I have said is somewhat proved—though what the meaning of the proof is—that, too, I do not know." She sighed, belched a little as she gazed at Siu-mei, and looked vacantly about the room. "I suffer a good deal now with my stomach," she said plaintively. "Nothing I eat feeds me." She wiped her mouth with her apron. "Tell me," she said, "is it true that a child like mine always kills its mother?"

"I don't know," Siu-mei said desperately. "Ask me nothing—leave me alone."

Ya-ching turned obediently and then stood at the door. "I have heard old women tell it so," she said sadly. "In one way or another, they say, such a child always kills its mother." She went away then, padding down the bare corridors in her cloth shoes. And Siu-mei sat staring at those things before her for a while, and biting her thumbnail until the quick began to bleed. Then she took up those things and put them in her bosom and rose from her chair.

"I must know the truth," she thought. "I must know it whatever it is."

Yasuda first, she made up her mind quickly. But she would find Sara to go with her for strength into Yasuda's presence. "Oh, I will tell her everything!" she thought. "I can bear it better if someone knows!"

But Sara was not in her rooms, and Sara was not in the garden. Sara was nowhere to be found; Siu-mei, searching one room after another, could not find her. Out in the side courtyard under an orange tree she found the amah and the baby, playing placidly in the mild air.

"Where is Durand doctor?" Siu-mei cried.

"She went out of the front gate after she ate this morning," the amah replied. She clucked at the baby proudly. "See this one's new tooth, Ling doctor! She bit a gash in my finger. Look!"

"Wicked one," Siu-mei said without looking. "Tell me, did Durand doctor go out all alone?"

"Alone," the amah replied.

"Carrying nothing?"

"Her medicine case, as she always does."

"And saying nothing?"

"Only to bid me squeeze an orange for this little meat dumpling when the sun is halfway between the wall and the top of the orange tree—oh, my mother, it is there now!" The amah rose and rushed away, the baby in her arms.

"She would go to the streets ruined yesterday," Siu-mei thought quickly. "She will be there, and I will find her." She ran across the court as she thought and saw Gray, walking slowly toward the hospital, his head bent.

"Why, he looks ill!" she thought. But she ran on, down the steps and out of the gate, and then in the street walked quietly and swiftly among the broken bricks and gaping holes. Working men were filling and mending, and they paused as she passed and then went on again.

But she had not far to go before she saw Sara, and with Sara a ragged, black-faced crowd of thirty or more men, women, and children. Ahead of them Sara marched, her face stern, her feet tempered to the shuffling, halting footsteps of those following her.

Siu-mei hurried to her. "Now what do you do?" she asked.

"These are our guests," Sara said firmly. "We have empty rooms and empty beds and idle hands, and this morning I could bear it no longer. I went out and found homeless ones."

They were beggars, Siu-mei saw quickly, the desperate poor, who do not care who feeds them or what shelters them. They were wounded, and some were burned in yesterday's great fire. These were they who lived in mat sheds, hovels which were gone in one instant's blaze.

"We'll fill the hospital somehow," Sara said recklessly.

"I can't stand it empty any more. I've got to have work."
She quickened her steps, and all the wretched crowd
gathered their rags together and hastened theirs.

"I have not eaten in four days," one muttered.

"I? I cannot count the days since I saw food," another
wailed.

"You will be fed," Sara promised.

Siu-mei fell in with her, and Sara seized her hand and
hand in hand they entered the hospital gate and the
crowd swarmed up the steps to the door.

"Now, Siu-mei," Sara said restlessly, "not a moment is
to be lost. There's a job here. Take them into the clinic
for preliminaries. There's smallpox among them, if I'm
not mistaken."

The door of Gray's office opened, and he stood there
staring. "My God!" he said.

"These are patients," Sara said with hard brightness.

"You went out and raked them in," he said.

Her lips quivered. "I have to work," she said plead-
ingly. His own white face made her heart ache. But she
was helpless to do anything for him, wasn't she? So she
must work.

He looked at her tender face. For a grown woman she
had the tenderest, most uncovered face he had ever seen.
That was because she never thought about herself or how
she looked.

"I'll be along," he said quietly, "in a moment."

He went back into his office and began to scrub his

hands. He need not tell her at once. Now he would put off telling her that he had decided to go away. There were all those people she had found, God knows where —wrecks of more than war. He sighed. Of course he'd have to tell her and tell her today. Louise was already looking up steamers and talking about a plane to take them out of Chen-li. He encouraged the idea of a plane grimly. There was always a good chance of those one-motored things cracking up against the mountains be-tween Chen-li and the sea. He dried his hands thor-oughly. Then he remembered Yasuda. He'd better just have a look at the fellow before he plunged into the human mess waiting for him in the clinic.

. . . Yasuda was sound asleep. Somehow he had sim-ply fallen asleep. For a moment he dreamed he was locked in the hideous semiconsciousness which followed the taking of the Chinese drug Chung had given him, when he could hear and understand what was going on, but could not speak. But now he felt curiously free. His breathing was easy and his muscles supple. He opened his eyes suddenly, aware of having been waked. A mo-ment before he had thought drowsily that someone was in the room, but then hearing nothing he had slept on. Now the door opened and shut and he heard it. Two people stood at his bed. He wet his dry lips with his tongue. Something was wrong. He felt perfectly well. The drug had not worked! He stared and saw the

Chinese female doctor and Thomison, the American, and he tried to smile.

"You are better this morning," Gray said in surprise.

"Much better," Siu-mei murmured. Her face went completely white. Then to her astonishment she felt her head whirl, the light of the morning went black before her eyes, and she fell across the bed.

"She has fainted," Yasuda cried. Without thinking what he did he leaped out of bed and in his hospital sleeping pajamas ran to the ewer and dipped a towel into the water and ran back to Siu-mei, clucking with his tongue against the roof of his mouth and wiping her face and slapping her hands with the wet end of the towel. It was done in an instant. Then he remembered himself. He stole a sick look at Gray. And he saw Gray standing there, tall and stern, the amazement on his face changing rapidly to certainty.

"You are very strong for a sick man, Mr. Yasuda."

Mr. Yasuda giggled. "I? Yes, please, thank you—" In his agitation his voice trailed off into a squeak. He looked at Siu-mei helplessly and saw her eyes beginning to open, and he threw the towel under the bed and crept into bed and pulled the covers up to his chin and lay looking at Gray, the frightened smile on his face.

Siu-mei struggled to her feet. "Oh," she sighed, "I never fainted before."

"You could not have chosen a better time," Gray said distinctly. "Come, let us go."

He took Siu-mei's arm as he spoke and led her to the door with him. Then he paused and took out the key. When they had gone out he paused once more and locked the door. Then he turned to Siu-mei.

"You had better go and rest," he said.

"I cannot," she replied. "I must tell you a matter. It is why I fainted—so stupidly, I know, but I could not believe—that he was all right. But he was."

"He certainly was," Gray said. "Come into my office, then." He led her into his office and closed the door and put her into an easy chair and poured some water into a glass and gave it to her.

"Tell me quietly and as you are able," he said.

She sipped the water a moment, then she put it down, and then, gathering together all the strength of her soul, she told Gray what Ya-ching had told her. She kept nothing back. Out of her bosom she took the two packages of pills and laid them on the table before him and the scrap of cloth torn from Chung Third's sleeve. Her tongue did not falter even over the name of her lover. And Gray listened without moving. What she was saying fitted with terrible precision into what he knew already. The hospital had not been bombed because Yasuda was here. Yasuda was kept here by Chung's keeping him ill. Then the sooner they got rid of Yasuda the better. But first this fellow Chung must be caught and turned over to the police. He looked sharply at Siu-mei.

"It is brave of you not to shield your betrothed," he

said. "I hesitate to say what ought to be done, knowing what your heart is."

But Siu-mei did not flinch under his keen eyes. "Why he should have done as he has, I cannot think," she said. "One would have said he had—everything—so that he needed nothing more. But he has chosen to be a traitor, and by his choice we are parted." Her voice was a whisper, but her face was proud and calm.

"Then," Gray said, "the sooner we send Yasuda away the better."

"Yes," she said.

"And he—Chung—he must be faced."

"Yes," she said again. Then her proud look broke. "I cannot—will you—I will go to the Eagle, Thomison doctor, and tell him that he can come for Yasuda if you will—go to Chung."

"Certainly I will," Gray said. "It is not fitting for you. But how can you go to the Eagle?"

"My father knows the way," she said. "He has been there, and he will go with me."

"Go, then," Gray said, "as quickly as you can."

"Now," Siu-mei said, "now—before *he* comes back. I must never see him again!"

"Now," Gray agreed.

She slipped from the room, and a few minutes later he saw her hurrying down the steps of the hospital and out of the great gate. Then he rose and picked up the packets of pills and put the ragged scrap in his pocket and went out and turned, not toward the clinic, but toward the laboratory. He would have the analysis of these pills made before Chung came back.

. . . In his bed Yasuda lay and sweated until he could bear it no more. Then he got up and tiptoed across the room to the door and tried it. It was locked, as he had feared. He strained at it, trying to make no noise, but it would not open, and he gave it up and prowled about the room. There was no other door, he knew, but what about partitions? Lathe and plaster would be easy to dig through, if not now then in the night. He tapped and felt. No, it was all solid brick, and he had no tool of any sort. He went to the window and looked out. The room was high up, and the court below was tiled. To leap would be folly if he broke only a leg; if worse, it would be a stupid way even to die. Better to take too many pills than lie mangled! He was a good Buddhist, and he respected the wholeness of the human body. So he went over to the drawer and took out the pills and poured them into his hand. There were only a few left, and as he examined them he saw at once that they were frauds. The real ones were hard pellets like clay. These he could crush— Who had done this? Chung—Chung had betrayed him! He heard a footstep, and he rushed back into his bed and feigned sleep. Someone tried the door, found it locked and went away. He opened his eyes and lay raging at Chung, the traitor. So all the time this Chinese had been betraying him while he took his money! All Chinese were liars and traitors! He would get out somehow and back to his own people and tell them that it was true, all Chinese were liars and traitors.

In his helpless rage he thought of his own country, his good faithful wife and his honorable old parents, his four little children and his lovely garden, and he began to sob. Perhaps he would never see them again. He had left them because it was his duty to obey the Emperor and fight, but always he longed to go back to them. He was a quiet good man and fond of his family, and he loved to arrange his garden. By this time he was wailing softly in a sort of madness of rage at Chung, who had betrayed him.

"It is your fault, sir," he said to an imaginary Chung standing before him. "If I am compelled to commit a crime and kill you, it is your fault and I am guiltless."

He sat up cross-legged on his bed and squared his elbows. His face was now the color of red wine. His eyeballs protruded with the force of his glare as he watched the door.

"I am a tiger trapped," he chanted softly, deliriously, "I am a strong Japanese tiger!"

. . . Chung ran up the steps of the hospital gaily. He had had an excellent feast. The wine was extraordinary. Besides, he had done what he had planned to do among his fellows. They had talked as sensible modern men.

231

Obviously it was impossible for a medieval country such as China was to win in this war. Obviously the Americans and Englishmen were glad to have them go on fighting merely to engage the Japanese. The patriotic duty of all far-seeing Chinese, therefore, was to make peace with Japan on any terms. He and Yasuda had talked this over clearly many times. Later, of course, though he never told this to Yasuda, when the Chinese were strong and thoroughly modernized, they would throw the Japanese out with all the other foreigners. He foresaw infinite possibilities ahead for power. To use people, that was the secret, he told himself, smoothing down his hair before the mirror in his office, to use people as he now used Louise and his brother and Ya-ching, and, for that matter, Yasuda himself. He thought with satisfaction of Siu-mei. In that day to come, when he was a powerful and important man, she would be worthy of a place beside him as his beautiful wife.

He left the office feeling very content with himself. This war, he was thinking, was actually turning to his advantage. He would go first to Yasuda and tell him how successful he had been in persuading his friends. So he went down the corridor and turned the handle of Yasuda's door, and to his surprise it was locked.

Who would lock this door? He had a master key on the key ring in his pocket, but he paused a moment before he used it and listened. Someone was in there with Yasuda. He heard low snarling murmuring talk. But what could this be? He turned the key quickly in the lock and went in.

Something sprang at him from the bed, a knot of concentrated fury flung against him, slammed the door shut behind him with its impact, and bore him down. He struggled against it, clawing and scratching and kicking, but the thing was digging in his entrails and clutching at his throat. Besides, he was soft with food and wine and lack of exercise. He was nothing before this ball of iron. He felt his head bent back between his shoulder blades and heard the loud click-clack of his own breaking neck. Then he knew no more.

. . . Ya-ching, coming back again to Yasuda's room, opened the door softly and saw that last backward thrust. She cried out, shut the door and locked it, and took away the key and ran through the corridors to the cubicle which was her own room. She did not hesitate for one moment. Chung was dead, so what reason had she now for accusation? What reason even to stay here any longer where he was not? She found a large blue cotton handkerchief, and into it she packed quickly all her belongings. There was almost nothing—her one good suit of dark clothes she put on. Her old mother had made them for her when she came to Chen-li to find work as a serving maid. They had told her here that foreigners paid good wages, and so she had come to the hospital and begun as a scrubbing woman. She had worn uniforms ever since except for the red silk gown she had bought to wear for *him*. She put this in hastily and her wooden comb and her foreign toothbrush, and then she tied the handkerchief and crept out, down the backstairs, out of the back court. Everybody was busy with the beggars Durand doctor had brought in. They had grown used to idleness in the hospital, and everybody was grumbling about having to clean and cook for beggars. She ran for the back gate and went out into the narrow alley that led to the street that went down to the river. There at the river it was easy to find a boat going up the rapids to the next town, and from there she could walk across country to her own village. What she would do then, she did not know. They would not welcome her nor the extra mouth she brought with her.

But she never reached her village. Who that had known Ya-ching could ever tell what became of her? The boat was crowded with people weary of the dangers of Chen-li. She had to squeeze herself into the edge of the crowd, and the boards of the small junk were slippery and wet. They said that the pock-marked girl sat on her bundle at the very edge of the deck, and there was nothing for her to hold when in the midst of the rapids the junk heaved to one side. She slipped off before any hand could catch her, and the rapids covered her. Useless it was to endanger them all by stopping in that dangerous place. Besides, who had courage to rescue a creature snatched away by the river god?

People looked at each other and murmured, "Doubtless she had committed some crime and the gods punished her."

"Doubtless it was so," they told each other, "a girl traveling alone, and with child."

They opened her bundle and looked, but there was nothing to tell her name, so what could they do with the garments except divide them? "I will take that red thing," a woman screamed, and she put out her strong brown arm and tore it out of the hands of three others. "Give me the handkerchief," a toothless old woman cried, so they let her have this last thing, and she took it and tied it over her head and was pleased. "The sun was hot on me," she remarked, "but the gods help the good."

. . . But Ya-ching's scream at his door had waked Yasuda out of his fury. He lifted his head, then he got up, trembling a little. He suddenly felt cold and weak. The Chinese was dead. He had not forgotten that trick of jujitsu, though when he had learned it as a young man he had never thought to use it on any human creature. But this he had been compelled to do. Had he not been compelled? He shivered and wondered. If he had not been a prisoner among enemies, it would not have been necessary. But when the one man whom he had trusted proved traitor, there was nothing to do but kill him.

"*Ah-mit-ah-ba!*" he murmured to Buddha.

Only now did it occur to him that this was the moment for escape. He tried the door—locked! But how could it be locked? It had been open, it must have been open when the Chinese came in. There had been no time for locking. In a fever he felt through Chung's clothing. There was no key—nothing but a letter. He threw the letter down, then picked it up again and put it in his pocket. It was one of the letters made ready for the white woman to copy. He had better keep it. So then he was still prisoner! And there was this body! His eyes ran over the small room. There was no place to hide the body. Then he thought of something. Chung's room was almost directly above his on the top floor. He could throw the body out of the window. It would fall upon the court below. Who would know from which window it had fallen when it lay crushed upon the tiles below, its neck broken?

Strong with his need, he lifted Chung's body, graceful even in death, the head hanging strangely like a flower broken at the stalk. He staggered to the window and looked out. There was not a person to be seen. It was time for the noon meal, the best possible time for what he had to do. He gathered himself together and flung the body out. It was gone. He heard in a small second the soft clattering crash below. Then he went over to his bed and climbed in and drew the covers up to his neck and closed his eyes. He was tired, mortally tired, with what he had had to do, and he was trembling again.

"For I am not a man of blood," he thought piteously.

"I am not accustomed to killing men, even righteously. Buddha, understand that I am a man of peace!"

Thus praying, he lay and thought of his garden and his little children and his wife and his old parents.

"Return me, O Buddha, in peace to those who wait for me!" And, thus praying, he waited.

. . . Upon the thousand stone steps of the mountain Siu-mei climbed steadily upward. Behind her the chairbearers swung her empty sedan chair. Never, they agreed, had they hired themselves better than to this girl who walked endlessly on her own two feet. Old Mr. Ling, sitting tilted up in his own sedan still further behind, watched Siu-mei anxiously.

"Spare yourself!" he called to her.

But she called back, "I am better if I am walking in this sun and wind!"

She went on steadily and he watched her, tenderness in his eyes. All would be well for this beloved child of his, he was thinking. The gods were knowing. They had ways to heal the hearts of the young and the good.

"Drink tea!" he called loudly at a small wayside tea shop tucked into the crevice of the cliff.

The chair coolies let him down grunting. "There is iron in this old sir," one said jovially to another. "I never knew a thin old man to weigh like a fat one before," another said.

Mr. Ling laughed and threw them some copper coins.

"I grow very heavy each time we come near a tea shop," he said. Then they all laughed.

Siu-mei, seating herself at one of the rough small bamboo tables, smiled without hearing. Mr. Ling sat down beside her and handed her his fan. The wind had suddenly died down.

"It must be well after noon," he said, squinting upward at the sun. "We will be there in another two hours."

She did not answer, and he sat peaceably drinking his tea. Whatever the gods designed, it was well. There was design in this moment upon the mountain, design, he thought, half-smiling, in the color that sun and wind were putting upon Siu-mei's cheeks. He looked at her, an old man long past caring for such things, but still he was pleased that his only daughter was very beautiful.

"She was too pale when she came home this morning," he thought, "but now by the time Chen-ta sees her she will be a pomegranate flower."

He sat placidly enjoying the beauty of the white-foamed stream rushing and falling beneath them and then enjoying the far beauty of the wide plains beyond, though all the time deeply aware of this young heart's distress beside him. But he could see the end to that distress, and it was not far off, though now to her it seemed so endless.

"I shall never marry," she had told him this morning sobbing. "I cannot love again!"

He smiled, looking out over plains. How could he tell her that the true tragedy was that love could always begin again and again?

So when in a few minutes she sprang to her feet, restless with present sorrow, he agreed amiably to go on. Chen-ta was on the mountaintop. Mr. Ling had made sure of that by a certain code he knew. In a watch-tower still standing in the ruined city wall of Chen-li he paid the guard to fly a green flag. When any saw this flag he sent word, mouth to ear, to Chen-ta, and Chen-ta came home to his mountain if he could. If he could a pillar of smoke went up from between the two great rocks that were the mountain crest. If he could not, there was no smoke. This morning the smoke rose quickly when the green flag flew. The Eagle was in the eyrie, and so Mr. Ling had set out at once, the sooner to ease his child's heart.

Now, seating himself in his sedan once more, he went on enjoying each fresh turn of the scene about him. Nor did he speak again to Siu-mei to beg her to ride. Sun and wind and mountain were doing their healing work, he saw, not only in the color upon her cheeks, but in the growing calmness of her eyes and the returning tranquillity of her lovely mouth. She could even smile when once he called her attention to a nest full of young birds in a clump of bamboos which they passed.

Not until they were within a mile of the mountaintop, then, did he call to her.

239

"Rest now, daughter. And mend your hair. The wind has blown it into a tangle. And a handsome young man is waiting up there."

He smiled at her, daring to tease her, and she caught that teasing look and turned away. But he was well pleased. For she obeyed him, and when the coolies lowered the chair she stepped in, and he saw her later when the gates of the Eagle's encampment were in sight, mending her hair and making it neat and looking at herself secretly in the mirror of a small foreign handbag she carried. He laughed to himself, the quiet laughter of a wise old man. In a few weeks, in a few days perhaps, when he teased her she would pout instead of turning away, and then when he teased her she would smile and then blush, and so a better love would begin. He felt wonderfully content.

"How well the gods manage for us all," he remarked to the universe about him.

. . . As for Chen-ta, he had had no idea of the fortune now drawing near him. He had come back to the mountain two days before, bringing all his men back with him to prepare for a great secret attack upon the enemy at a spearhead they had made by pushing into a village within twenty miles of Chen-li. He was putting all his strength into this attack, and his eyes were on Chung Third night and day. It would have been easy to have the man killed, but foolish, for while he was alive and free he would reveal the whole of what Chen-ta now suspected to be a vast secret. So he kept the man alive and near him so he could not run away and sweating with uncertainty and fear.

Thus when the green flag flew the Eagle was there on his mountain, and now his men, always watchful on the path, sent word that guests were coming—two sedans. They were at first still too far off to see who they were, so he waited in his main court, eating oranges and drinking wine. Then it was told him who they were.

"The honored old Ling," his man said, scraping the dust with his bare toe, "and his daughter."

"Not that one herself!" he shouted.

"Which?" the man said stupidly.

"The beautiful one, fool!" Chen-ta bellowed.

"This is one certainly worth a man's eyes," the man retorted, "for I saw her myself."

Chen-ta leaped to his feet and ran for his own rooms. "And I sitting here like a lout!" he roared, "in dust and dirt and orange skins!"

He yelled for hot water and foreign soap and for his barber and for his good new clothes and leather shoes and his new wrist watch he had taken from a Japanese captain not long since, and everybody ran about to serve him, thinking him mad.

But he had himself clean and at his best in the little time left, and the courtyard swept and new tea and wine and little cakes ready, and when it was cried at the gates that they were come, he stood up and the sun shone on his dark handsome face and he looked like a king.

"Like a king," Mr. Ling thought. But he did not say so. He merely came forward, walking in the swaying way that old scholars walk, his robes swinging from side to side, to make his greeting. And when this was done he nodded to Siu-mei as at some small thing he had brought along.

"This one," he said to the Eagle, "is my solitary, negligible child whom you have seen."

Then he stepped back to enjoy himself. And what he enjoyed were these two, standing face to face, looking at each other, as if for the first time they saw what they were.

X

Now the Eagle had ready in his mind the greetings he would give to this girl, or thought he had. He had planned to say, "This place is not worthy of you," or "Deign to rest yourself in my hovel, unworthy as it is." But instead of these courteous words he blurted what was in his mind.

"Why have you come—to me?"

Siu-mei blushed and bowed her head to hide it. "I am angry," she thought, and tried to be angry. "Only on business," she said haughtily. "I come for the American, Thomison."

"Do not talk business before you have eaten and rested," Chen-ta said. He was cursing himself for his bluntness. Who was he to say such a thing to a beautiful girl, a girl learned in ways in which he was ignorant? Yet to be ashamed of himself was such a new thing to the Eagle that now he was abashed still further. Never, he told himself, could he make amends for this coarse beginning. He turned abruptly and led the way into the main hall.

Now Siu-mei saw his shame and shyness, and at once she began to like him. The small anger she had tried to foster went away altogether. She waited decorously while her father sat down in the chief seat and then, obeying Chen-ta's invitation, she bowed and sat down.

"If you will allow me," she began directly, "I will speak at once. We must start back before it grows late."

"Speak, then," Chen-ta said, but to himself he vowed that it would be too late before they could start, and they must stay until tomorrow.

So Siu-mei began, looking at her father now and again to catch his nod at what she said. But the rest of the time she talked she looked quietly and directly at Chen-ta, thinking altogether of what she was saying, and yet seeing, too, that bold and eager face of his.

"The American, Thomison, sent me," she repeated. This young man must understand that she did not seek him out of her own will. "Strange things are at our hospital. We cannot understand their meaning. But now at least it is partly clear that the center of what happens is your captive, the Japanese, Yasuda. You remember you brought him with a belly wound."

"Which I made," Chen-ta said calmly.

"It healed within a few weeks," she went on. "Then you came for him."

"He was ill then of another disease," Chen-ta broke in, "and every time since he has had that illness."

"We have now found what it is," Siu-mei said. "He has been taking a poison."

"Poison!" Chen-ta cried. He leaned forward and put his hands on his knees and stared at her.

"That he might escape you and remain in the hospital," Siu-mei said. She wet her lips. Now was the time that she must tell the whole of it, all that she knew, even of Chung, "he who can be no more to me," she thought, her heart quivering.

"That is not all," she said resolutely. "There is a Chinese who helped him—who gave him the drug—the Chinese, Chung En-liu, the house doctor of our hospital."

Over Chen-ta's face came a still look. He did not move. Old Mr. Ling, watching, began to stroke his beard. Siu-mei's eyes turned away from Chen-ta's face.

"You will say, why did this Chinese give a drug to a Japanese? Who can say what is in a heart? But if there is any plan between a Chinese and a Japanese today, it can be only evil. That is known."

"That is known," Chen-ta repeated in a low voice.

"Yet what the plot is, we cannot fully see," Siu-mei said, "except that somehow it must be linked with this —since Yasuda has eaten the drug the enemy planes have passed over the hospital. We have been as safe as though we were in a foreign country. The people have hated us and suspected us. I have feared even for the lives of the Americans if it continued. But my father is one of the elders in Chen-li, and he has counseled patience to all who inquired of him."

Chen-ta's eyes were now beginning to grow large with anger and surprise. He opened his mouth to speak, but Siu-mei put up her pretty hand.

"Wait—there is a little more." She put her hand to her mouth a moment, thinking whether she must speak of Ya-ching and of that private sorrow of her own love, and went on without deciding. Let her words come as they must, she told herself. "There is a nurse at the hospital who told me that a younger brother of Chung En-liu brings him messages. These messages are like this—'The Sha-wu mountains.'"

Now Chen-ta could bear no more. He leaped to his feet and in three steps was out of the hall and in the courtyard roaring for his guard. Three men came running like rabbits.

"Fetch me that Chung Third!" he bellowed.

"Sir, he went down the mountain," one of the guard said timidly. "He said his mother was dying."

Chen-ta ground his teeth. "When did he go?"

"When the guests came in, he went out," another faltered.

"And did none stop him or ask him if he had my consent?" Chen-ta shouted.

"Sir, he said he did not like to trouble you when you

had guests. He said for one of us to tell you—and that assuredly he would be back early in the morning."

"Go after him," Chen-ta broke in. "Do not return without him. If you cannot find him, go to his home and bring all his family here in his stead until he is found!"

"So! So! So!" The three men ran off as fast as feet could go.

And Chen-ta strode about the court a few times and then went back into the hall and sat down.

"Go on," he said to Siu-mei.

"I have told you the most of it," Siu-mei replied.

"This nurse," Chen-ta said, considering, "why should she accuse Chung Third? What business had she with him?"

Thus sharply he plucked out the one thing Siu-mei had not told him. So she told him that, too, for suddenly she wanted him to know everything.

"She was with child," she said in a low voice, "and she hated the man, for he would not marry her and she wanted to injure him. So, having by chance seen Chung Third coming secretly to his brother's room by night, she suspected evil. And so she watched and caught the younger brother that she might have a weapon against— the elder." Her voice fell still lower.

"He!" Chen-ta said softly.

"He," Siu-mei said steadily.

They looked at each other, these two, and when she

saw understanding and pity and admiration come dawning over his face, her eyes filled with tears, and she turned away her head.

"He is nothing to me—now," she whispered.

Old Mr. Ling coughed. Now it was time to come forward and delay a little this headlong falling into love. Nothing should move too quickly to its end.

"Sir," he said to the Eagle, "you have the matter before you. It now remains only for you to take back your captive. By now the American has turned over the traitor Chung to the police. He was to do that while we came to you to tell you and to ask that the Japanese be taken away. There is no use in cleaning away a cobweb if the spider is not removed also."

"I will remove him," Chen-ta said. "Do not fear. But not while the worm of a younger brother is not found." He rose and clapped his hands for a servant, and he said to Siu-mei tenderly, "Now you are very weary. Go to an inner room and waiting women will serve you. Eat a little hot food they have ready for you, and sleep."

"It will be too late—" she began, looking at her father.

"You will not leave the mountain tonight," Chen-ta said. "At dawn, I promise, you may go if you wish."

So firm and quiet was his voice that to her own surprise Siu-mei yielded to it. She turned to her father and found him nodding acquiescence.

"I myself am very tired," the old man said.

So she followed the servant through two courts and

candlelight, thinking. "There is one more not yet found," he mused to himself. "This traitor to the other traitor, and that one to the Japanese. But where is the one between him and the enemy to whom he belongs?" He pondered this a long time and then he gave a shout of command. A guerrilla sprang into the light around him.

"Order a band of fifty within an hour," Chen-ta said. "We go to the city to bring back my prisoner. He is healed."

"So!" the man shouted. He disappeared to obey, and Chen-ta rose to go and change his garments for the journey. If all went well, he would be here again at dawn, ready when she awoke.

. . . Louise, in the afternoon of that day, came tripping along the brick path toward the hospital and stopped to twist off the low branch of a blooming magnolia. She felt so gay, so joyous, so good, she thought, now that Gray had yielded. She would take the branch of magnolia to Yasuda. He was so appreciative of her.

"I really feel myself," she thought, "as though I could be the sort of person I truly am. Gray hasn't really *seen* me."

She tripped along again, holding the spray of great white flowers carefully. "I'm rather nice," she thought complacently, "if I am given a chance to be!"

A week from today at most, and she would never see any of this again, never, never! She looked about the compound as she went. It had never looked so neat as it had before the old gardener was killed. Well, some day they might all thank her that he was the last one that had been killed! Her mind went for a moment to Chung. It was strange that he had not brought her a letter for several days. She must ask Gray if he were ill or away—not that she cared. She would be glad to get out of whatever she was in, though nothing—nobody—would ever get her to say—to believe—that she had done anything wrong in making them all *safe*.

And then she saw something, lying in a crumpled heap on the tiles. It was a man, she saw at once. Then she saw who it was—Chung! His head was bleeding and crushed, but the face was clear and unharmed. She gave a great scream and threw away the branch she held. It fell, as though she had meant it, across his twisted body, but she did not heed it. She ran across the court, up the steps, screaming, "Gray—Gray—oh, Gray—oh, Gray, where are you?"

But he, far off in the laboratory, did not hear. Mind and heart were absorbed. Out of the hard pills he had isolated, after two hours, a strange substance he did not know. It was like digitalis, but it was not like it, either. A derivative of foxglove base, perhaps, of which digitalis was the derivative. But in any case a powerful and depressing drug, acutely dangerous except in these minute doses. Ah, but Chung was too clever! This was an ancient Chinese poison, doubtless. He knew his own knowledge of poisons slight, but he had heard endless stories from his patients of poisons so subtle that they caused anything from constant headache to sudden death.

But Sara heard that screaming high voice, and she ran out from the clinic to find its cause. Louise stared at her, stumbled and caught herself on Sara's shoulder.

"Oh, it's Chung—he's dead!"

Sara shook her hard. "Be quiet—where?"

"He's fallen—out in the court—his head!" Louise panted, shuddered, and pointed toward the court, and Sara ran out and down the steps and saw for herself that crumpled heap. To it she stooped and pulled away the magnolia branch—who had put it there?—and then saw that Chung was dead, indeed. There could be no doubt. His neck was broken, his skull cracked. She hesitated, feeling herself grow giddy. Then she steadied herself, took off her white surgeon's apron and covered him. Gray must be told at once. She had not allowed herself to go near Gray all morning, and yet she had been constantly aware of his absence, that he had not come to the clinic as he had said he would. Now she must go to him. And Siu-mei—where was she? She hurried back into the hall. Louise was leaning against the wall, very white.

"I'm going to be sick," she gasped.

"Go into my office and lie down on the couch." Sara flung the words over her shoulder and hurried on.

But Gray, Gray, where was he? She could not find

him in his office, in the men's hospital, anywhere. Then she thought of the laboratory, and there he was, his face grave over a retort he held in his hand as she threw open the door.

"Gray, here you are!" she cried.

He looked at her. "I was just coming to tell you some bad news," he said guardedly.

"But I have dreadful news," she said. "Chung is dead! Gray, he must have—killed himself. He's lying in the court, beneath his window."

"Dead!" Gray cried. He put down the retort. "Then there's no use my going on. I suppose he must have found out—somehow—that he was discovered."

"What, Gray?" She came close and stared at the retort.

"That," he said. "It's poison. He had been feeding it to Yasuda, just enough to keep him down."

"Gray! Why?"

"To keep him in the hospital, for some reason."

"You don't think it was just so we couldn't be bombed?"

"I think it must have been something beyond that," Gray said. He strode toward the door with her as he spoke. "Chung wasn't a physical coward. He was too cool-headed. No, there was something else. I wonder if now we will ever know."

She followed him out of the side door of the hospital and beckoned orderlies as they went out. By now a small crowd had gathered around the dead man. Others had found him and cried out when they saw the doctors coming. Gray bent and examined the body quickly.

"He has been dead for some little time," he said to Sara. He nodded to the orderlies and waited until they had lifted their burden. Then he turned to Sara and walked with her into the hospital.

"I suppose Siu-mei must be called," Sara said.

"Eh?" Gray started. "Oh, I forgot. No! See here, Sara, I was just about to come and tell you, but I thought I'd get my proof ready first in the laboratory."

They were in the office now, and he closed the door. His voice was quiet and his mind and hers absorbed, and yet each was acutely remembering what had happened in this very room only yesterday. Then, being what they were, they put themselves aside. Gray sat down, facing her across his desk.

"Siu-mei brought me these pills this morning with a strange story. Ya-ching had been giving them—under Chung's orders, of course. It's fearfully complicated. Ya-ching was in love with Chung. It was all right as long as he treated her well, it seems. That is, she obeyed him. Then—he got her with child."

"Gray! I can't believe what you're telling me!"

"It's true, I'm afraid. And he wouldn't marry her, naturally, being engaged to Siu-mei. And Ya-ching turned against him and substituted some pills she made herself—harmless, of course, and so had the proof. And she brought it all to Siu-mei."

"Oh, poor Siu-mei!" Sara's vivid face was misery.

"Siu-mei was simply tops," Gray said. "We agreed that the first thing to do was to get Yasuda away."

"Why on earth didn't she let me help in all this?" Sara cried.

"She did go to find you and found you out collecting beggars," Gray said with a quick smile, "and so she came to me. And she said if I'd talk with Chung she'd go to the Eagle and have him come for Yasuda. That's where she is now—her father's with her." He looked at his watch. "Four o'clock—they must be there." He sighed. "Well, I don't have to tell Chung. I'm sorry—and glad."

Gray's face set. There was that other thing that he must tell Sara, but he put it aside. Certainly he could not leave her now, with all this. He would simply have to tell Louise that their going was postponed and bear her disappointment as best he could. "I'll have to stand by Sara for a while," he would tell her. "After that—"

Across his thoughts Sara's voice broke timidly. "Gray, perhaps I ought to tell you something."

"What?" He looked up, half hearing out of his own thoughts.

"I don't know how to tell you."

He was surprised at her faltering, she who was so sure and quick. "Why, Sara, you and I—tell each other, don't we?" He could not keep his true heart out of his voice, his eyes. "We're always honest with each other, aren't we?"

"Too honest, perhaps, Gray!"

"There's no such thing possible between us," he retorted, and waited, compelling her with his eyes upon her.

She lifted her own bravely. "It's about Louise—that's why I don't know."

"What about Louise?" His voice was curt.

"Siao Fah came to me last night and said she was still getting those letters—Chung brought them, and Siao Fah posted letters of hers with Chinese stamps."

"He can't bring any more."

"No." She paused. No, she could not tell him the rest.

"What else?"

"The rest has nothing to do with—Chung."

"Tell me," he insisted.

"Gray, please—no."

"You must—everything has to be told now."

"Then—Gray, Siao Fah said he saw Harry Delafield take her in his arms."

"When?"

"Yesterday afternoon. He told me last night."

"But last night she told me—" he began and then stopped himself. No, he would wait. If Louise had been cheating, then no promises held! "I'll go to her myself," he said, leaping to his feet.

"Gray, she's in my office!"

"In your office?" He paused, amazed.

"Gray, did I forget to tell you? She found Chung first!"

"Louise?"

"Yes!"

They stared at each other uncertainly.

"Did she seem to be frightened?"

"Gray, I don't know—she said she felt sick. But that was natural."

He left her abruptly and she waited, listening to his footsteps, quick and firm. She waited and after a long time, but perhaps it was not long, because every instant of waiting was so long, he came back with Louise.

It was impossible to tell anything from Louise's face. She was so pretty, so calm.

"Just tell Sara what you've told me, please, Louise," Gray said sternly.

Louise lifted her eyebrows. "There's nothing to tell, Gray. Just that I was bringing some flowers over, as I do nearly every day. I'd just picked a branch of magnolias to give to Yasuda and then I saw—*him*—Chung."

"Was that how the magnolias happened to be there?" Sara cried.

"Where?" Gray asked.

"On—the body," Sara said.

"I threw them, I was so frightened," Louise said.

258

"They happened to fall like that, and then I couldn't bear to pick them up again."

Gray was frowning. "Louise, I've been waiting to hear one thing you haven't told."

Louise opened her golden eyes wide. "I've told you everything, Gray!"

"Not quite, Louise." Gray's voice was very quiet. "There s still something; it has worried me a long, long time."

Now she began to look frightened, Sara thought. There was the slightest flicker of the long lashes over those eyes.

"I can't imagine what, Gray," Louise said. She brushed a little thread from her skirt and crossed her pretty legs.

Gray's eyes grew hard as he watched her. "Then I'll tell you, Louise. I've known for a long time that Chung was bringing you letters from someone, and you were writing letters to someone, and Siao Fah has been mailing them."

Now anyone could see she was frightened.

"But, Gray, how absurd!" Her eyes went from Gray to Sara and back to Gray again. Her mind, running about like a wild thing caught, searching for escape. "But Chung's dead—he can't tell!" she was thinking.

"Siao Fah has seen it a good many times," Gray said slowly.

Louise's red lips quivered. "But, Gray darling, you wouldn't take a servant's word against mine? And you know Siao Fah always has been jealous of me with you. He'd like to make you hate me. I've tried to be patient, but I'm sure that's true."

He could not deny that, Gray thought. The quivering pretty lips did not touch his heart any more, but he was just and he must be just now, even to Louise—no, especially to Louise.

"That's true," he said to Sara.

Sara did not speak. She could not come between these two.

Gray lifted his head. "Siao Fah said you and Delafield kissed each other yesterday."

"What if we did?" Louise said. "It was nothing—he's going away. I'm fond of him. But that's all."

There was silence after that. Louise broke it by jumping to her feet.

"If you two have no more accusations, I'll go."

"Wait!" It was Gray's command.

Louise stopped, carefully patient with him.

"I think we'll go and see Yasuda. It just occurs to me. I left him locked up."

"Locked up!" Louise cried.

"Come," Gray said.

Louise hesitated. "I don't know that I—"

"Come!" Gray repeated sternly.

She shrugged and followed him, and Sara went behind her.

They went down the corridors and paused before

Yasuda's door. Gray tried it. It was still locked. He took the key from his pocket and opened the door and went in, half expecting in this strange day to see Yasuda gone. But he was there. He lay stretched straight in his bed, his eyes open and watchful.

"Mr. Yasuda," Gray said, "you are still better than you were this morning."

Mr. Yasuda did not answer. His eyes were fastened on Gray's face.

"In fact, you are well," Gray said abruptly. "I am preparing to discharge you."

Mr. Yasuda's lips barely moved. "When?"

"As soon as you are called for," Gray replied. He stood at Yasuda's side now, looking down on him.

Mr. Yasuda's lips barely moved again. "The guerrilla?" he asked.

"Exactly," Gray said. "After all, you are his prisoner. And he says he will not kill you—he has a use for you, he says."

"What use?" Mr. Yasuda's voice was dead in its faintness.

"That he did not tell me."

Mr. Yasuda thought rapidly. Until today he would have said that to be returned to his captor would be the worse fate in life. But now a worse might befall him. Here in the midst of enemies, if it were somehow known that he had killed a Chinese, though Buddha knew only righteously, how could he hope to escape death himself? He might escape somehow, if he were taken away from here.

"I will go," he said to Gray.

"But there is a question we must ask you," Gray said. Mr. Yasuda did not move.

"Mr. Yasuda, why did you willingly take that dangerous drug?"

"What drug?" Mr. Yasuda asked.

"The one given you by Doctor Chung, who was found dead a little while ago in the courtyard below these windows."

Mr. Yasuda's heart went mad in his breast. It was known—was it known? He choked back a wild fury of self-defense. Perhaps only accidentally had the American said "these windows."

He swallowed and wiped his lips with a furtive hand. "Doctor Thomison, you remember the saying of your people—all is fair in love and war. This is war."

"Go on," Gray said.

Mr. Yasuda went on, "I think I am not to be blamed too much if I endeavored—as a Japanese—to go on helping my country, though I am a prisoner. Therefore when I found a Chinese who would accept a recompense, I used him."

"For what?" Gray's question was a dagger thrust.

Mr. Yasuda did not evade it. "Frankly, to convey to my General valuable information."

"Concerning?"

"The plans of the guerrillas."

Louise sat down suddenly. "Gray, darling, I know this is wonderful intrigue and all that, but honestly I don't feel a bit well. I think I'll go home."

Gray turned the face of a stranger to her. "Sit there," he said. "Mr. Yasuda, how did you find out the plans of the guerrillas?"

Mr. Yasuda prayed, closing his eyes a moment. "Guide me, Buddha!" Then he opened his eyes again. In that instant he had a direct inspiration. He was not speaking to enemies, he was speaking to persons who were foreigners in this country like himself. So he would offer them his simple grateful friendship. He smiled eagerly.

"When you come to Japan, Doctor Thomison, my people will welcome you. They will treat you very well in appreciation for your great kindness to me. You have healed me and cared for me with such courtesy. And Mrs. Thomison has so kindly forwarded my letters—"

Gray bent over him. "Letters?"

"Yes, letters, like this." And Mr. Yasuda pulled from the pocket of his hospital pajamas the letter he had taken from Chung's body and held it out to Gray. "If you will send this, please? It is in code, of course—quite senseless unless you know it."

Gray took it. "Thank you," Mr. Yasuda said. "I hope the safety of the hospital has been something, Doctor Thomison, but I assure you my government will wish to give you a very substantial reward."

Gray straightened himself. "Come, Louise," he said.

Mr. Yasuda gazed, astonished. They were leaving him in the middle of what he was saying. They were locking the door on him again. Americans—they were incomprehensible!

Outside the door the three stood. Gray had taken hold of Louise's arm, and she tried to pull away.

"Gray, you hurt me!" she cried.

He did not hear her. He said to Sara, "Let me know when the Eagle comes."

She nodded. Could she speak or not? She despised Louise, and yet she pitied her at this moment. "Gray," she breathed.

He turned.

"Don't—be hard. We must be fair, you know, to everybody."

"Of course," he said shortly.

She watched him lead Louise away, Louise, his wife. She went back then to her office. The Eagle would be here surely before long. That split crest of mountain she could see black against the sky was only a few hours away, and he would make haste. She stood looking over the city. There had been no raid today. Then doubtless there would be one tomorrow. She sighed and felt unutterably weary and lay down upon her couch to think of Gray and of what he must be doing. Yet she could only wait.

. . . In his house Gray read the senseless letter aloud, slowly and distinctly.

Dear Harry:
I am much better, but still not well. There is a strong wind from the south and I have not been able to go out yet. But I hope to go out about noon.

He tore it to pieces. They stood, facing each other.

"Well?" Louise said harshly.

He did not answer. She flung herself into a chair.

"I suppose you'll never understand why I did it!"

Still he could not answer.

"You may not believe me, Gray, but honestly I thought it was the only way to save our lives!"

Then he found he could speak. "There's a plane going out about six in the morning."

"Gray, you mean—"

"I want you to take it."

"Gray, aren't you—"

"No, I'm staying. I want you to go."

She lit a cigarette, trying not to tremble. "Does this mean—"

"Anything you like," he said.

"Well!" she cried shrilly. "Well, of all things!"

"I'll—I'll go back to the hospital now," he said. "There's no one on night duty in the men's ward. I'll be back in time to take you to—to the port." He turned, and she flung at him all her fury.

"Of course I know why you're going back to the hospital, my dear Gray! Duty, tommyrot! You're going back to Sara—why don't you tell me the truth?"

"All right," he said, "I'm going back to Sara." He closed the door between them.

. . . But he did not go back to Sara. He went back to his own office; and Sara, lying acutely awake, heard him close his door and did not move. Of course he could not stay in that sad house of his tonight. She did not go to him, knowing that tonight each must be alone. But she rose, restless with his nearness, and went to the window and sat looking out over the city again, waiting, waiting.

It was long past midnight when the Eagle came. She heard the clatter of horsemen at the gate, and then the gate was thrown open and by the light of candle lanterns she saw the vague shapes, and then one shape, the Eagle, and behind him three men. She went out to open the door to him. He bowed to her quickly.

"Where is my prisoner?"

"Ready," she said. She led him to Gray's door, and when Gray came out she left them and went back to her office.

"Is the man well?" the Eagle asked of Gray.

"He is well," Gray replied. They walked on, and at Yasuda's door he paused. "You will not wantonly kill this man when I have given him to you?"

"I told you, I have my use for him," the Eagle said impatiently.

They went in and without a word Gray helped Yasuda to rise and dress and wrapped his greatcoat about him. And Yasuda, very pale, asked nothing. When he was ready the Eagle shouted, and the three men lifted Yasuda and carried him away. Then the Eagle looked at Gray.

"Is there anything you would say to me?" he asked.

"Nothing," Gray replied. "Whatever was is now finished." He hesitated, his conscience nagging him. Then he said unwillingly, "And yet, I suppose I ought to tell you that this man has while he was here found means to send information to his own people concerning you."

"I know," the Eagle said. "And shall I still not kill him?"

"Do not ask me," Gray said. "Or tell me," he added.

"Farewell, then."

"Farewell."

He watched the Eagle stride away. Then he looked about the empty room, the tossed bed. What had happened here, none would ever wholly know. He went back to his office, hesitating at the door. The light was burning down the hall in Sara's office. But no, it was too soon. They must work a while together—days, and weeks—months perhaps, before he could feel healed. He went into his own room. He would rest awhile and then make his rounds again.

. . . Dawn came, and Gray went to his house, dreading the necessity to see Louise, to speak to her. He might, even, have to waken her. But when he opened the door he saw there was no need for this. Siao Fah had discovered that Louise was going, and he was in a fury of housecleaning. He had tied dish towels around his head and Little Pig's, and in the living room they were scrubbing the floor, the rug rolled back and buckets of soapy water standing everywhere.

"Why do you clean at this hour?" Gray asked.

"It will take us all day to get this house as it should be," Siao Fah answered with pleasure plain on his face. He kicked Little Pig gently in the buttocks. "Clean under that table," he ordered.

To all this Louise's door was shut—locked, Gray found, when he tried the handle.

"Louise," he called softly.

"In a moment," she called back clearly.

And in a moment she opened the door wide and stood there, dressed to go.

"I'm taking only my two small bags," she said. "The rest you can send after me."

"Yes," he said gently, "I will."

Siao Fah leaped up. "Carry the bags!" he yelled at Little Pig. And Little Pig lugged the bags out to the gate. From somewhere Siao Fah had hired a ragged horse carriage to take them to the port, and now he came out to tell the driver where to go.

"Turn to the right when you leave the city gate," he bawled happily, "follow the river down and then, before

you get to the foreign oil tanks, turn left by a small
Earth God temple and go three sides of a square as the
road goes and there is the airfield, and you are the son
of a turtle if you get there too late for this white woman
to go away, and I will hold back your pay if she is not
gone!"

"I will swear to see her gone," the driver replied.

So Siao Fah and Little Pig stood staring while the carriage rattled off. And all the miles of that rough journey
Louise did not speak nor did Gray. There was nothing
left to say between them. He wondered if her breast
was full of despair as his was, but he could not tell. Her
look was hard and bright and never toward him.

At the airport three of the port men had come to see
her off, and he was thankful for their presence. They
made it possible to listen, to smile a little, to let the
stream of Louise's nervous banter with them run on.

"Oh, now, I don't believe you will miss me! What? I
don't want to come back, ever! I hope Gray will come
home to me." She flung a bright hard look at him. But
he did not answer. She had kept herself bright and hard
through all the parting, and he accepted it. Neither had
spoken to the other out of any depth. He had scarcely
spoken at all except the barest inquiries. "Sure you have
all the money you need?"—"Yes—plenty, thanks."—
"You'd better take the steamer rug."

Now the plane was ready. She was going aboard and
she turned and flung her arms about his neck.

"Good-by, darling!" Her bright hard face, the cool kiss, the sharp clear voice, the pretty head so high—did any wound bleed within? It was impossible to tell. She was gone.

He turned away with brief nods to the men and climbed into a riksha to go home again, to the hospital. Yes, that was home. He rode along the cobbled jarring road, not feeling, not thinking, only knowing that he was going home.

He was perhaps half a mile from the hospital when he heard the siren sound out sharply urgent.

"Let me down," he cried to his puller. "I will go the rest of the way on foot. You must seek shelter."

The man let him down at once and took his pay. "I ask forgiveness," he said apologetically, "but I have an old mother who cannot walk, and I pull her to the foot of the cliff and carry her up on my back to the shelters."

"Run!" Gray cried.

He ran himself. The siren was sounding again insistently. The enemy must have come by surprise. He ran, turning and twisting through short cuts and alleyways, and pushed open the hospital gates. Yasuda was gone! Was the evil peace gone with him? But would they know? The letter Yasuda had written he had torn and thrown away. Would they suspect that the plot had been discovered? Who could tell? He rushed panting into the hospital to find Sara already moving her beggars to the shelter.

"I couldn't take a risk," she told him. "They *might,* you know, today!"

"Right!" he agreed.

They were working together again in the old swift unison, too busy to think, too busy to suffer, working like one pair of hands together, like one brain.

"At least there are no sure-to-dies," she said, when the last beggar had been sent to shelter.

"What about us?" he asked.

"Shelter," she said quickly. He took her hand and they ran. "After all, we're important!"

He let her hand go until they were in the darkness of the cave. Then he took it again. They waited, hand in hand, the shapes of the beggars dim around them.

"If there is bombing near us, hold down your heads, close your ears and open your mouths," Gray ordered them.

"We know, foreign doctor," voices answered him. "We know, we know very well!"

"Poor things, so they do," Sara whispered.

They waited. The zooming grew loud and roared over them.

"They're passing!" she cried.

"No!" he shouted. "Wait!"

They waited an instant more, and then he pulled her over.

"They're over us, Sara!" he cried triumphantly. "They're bombing us."

They bent their heads among those others, no whit different at last, except that in the hideous thunder hand clung to hand closer than two hands could cling that had not lived and worked as these two had, together.